Copyright © 2021 Seb Duncan.

All rights reserved. No part of this publication may be reproduced, distributed, or transmitted in any form or by any means, including photocopying, recording, or other electronic or mechanical methods, without the prior written permission of the publisher, except in the case of brief quotations embodied in critical reviews and certain other non-commercial uses permitted by copyright law. For permission requests, write to the publisher, addressed "Attention: Permissions Coordinator," at the email address below.

Any references to historical events, real people, or real places are used fictitiously. Names, characters, and places are products of the author's imagination.

Front cover image: There Is Strong Shadow Where There Is Much Light, © Magnus Gjoen 2021

First printing edition 2021.

seb.of.duncan@gmail.com

Table of Contents

Chapter 1 The shop 1
Chapter 2 The Investigation 3
Chapter 3 Frosty Jacks - Breakfast of Champions 6
Chapter 4 The Hotel Room 9
Chapter 5 The Meeting 11
Chapter 6 The Auction 16
Chapter 7 Black Eye 20
Chapter 8 The Visitor Centre 23
Chapter 9 Old Town Square Investigation 25
Chapter 10 Operation Fake Head 27
Chapter 11 The Chrudim Investigation 29
Chapter 12 The Bowling Alley 41
Chapter 13 The Evidence 44
Chapter 14 Campaign Update 47
Chapter 15 The Book 49
Chapter 16 Fake Head Phase Two 53
Chapter 17 The Barn at Chrudim 59
Chapter 18 The Rabbit Hole 62
Chapter 19 Return of the Jan 69
Chapter 20 The Hotel 79
Chapter 21 The Hospital 82
Chapter 22 Film School 85
Chapter 23 Charles Bridge 89

HEADCASE

Seb Duncan

*Charles bridge stretched out in front of him.
It was as if he was walking out of the open mouth
of a fantastical creature.
The foggy cobbled road like the tongue,
the statues on either side like rows of jagged teeth
silhouetted against the blood red sunset.*

Prague 1582

It was a crisp early morning in September and the year is 1582. Jan Mydlár began the journey to start his medical degree at the prestigious Saint Wenceslaus College in Prague. With a proud heart, he thought of how his father, a town clerk, was thinking about him on this day. His father's dream was for his son to become the City Physician of their hometown, Chrudim. This day marked the first step in the realisation of that dream.

But Jan had dreams of his own. He also promised (to himself, at least) that on his return, he would marry his beloved Dorota, a secret love that even she was unaware of.

Smiling, Jan breathed in the cold bright air. Today was a good day. He could see the years stretching out ahead of him. Beyond the bleak horizon of morning. Beyond even his own hopes and dreams. Today was the beginning of forever...

Dorota

I first met my beloved Dorota through my "uncle". Master Mathew Mydlár was a distant relative on my father's side. After I had become a Latin scholar through my school studies, Uncle Mathew had asked me to help him to learn the language, and as a result we had struck up a friendship over the months of my tuition. What also grew was my love for his daughter. Although Uncle Mathew and I got on well, the real reason for my visits was to see Dorota. Every Wednesday my heart would skip as I entered the grand gates of Uncle Mathew's old house in the hope that I would see her. As a result, our relationship also became close as the classes progressed and my intentions towards her were hard to hide. I was relieved when he informed me that he would be happy for his daughter to marry a Physician such as I was to become. The day he informed me of this was a day I'll never forget, and I almost flew home on wings of joy at the thought of marrying her.

News from Chrudim

In the first year of my degree, I was absorbed in my studies. I had the privilege of being instructed by some of the most distinguished men of medical science. However, I still had the distraction of Dorota on my mind every day and had even started to write poems about her, much to the amusement of my fellow students.

Summer seemed to arrive very fast and I headed back home for the holidays. After seeing my parents, I rushed over to see Uncle and his daughter. They welcomed me back home with a warm embrace and Dorota complimented me on how handsome I had become. Uncle was interested in how Prague had changed since he had been there, as ill health had prevented him from being able to see the city for the past year. My stories of the city and the Latin lessons were a welcome distraction for him at this time.

My second-year summer holiday was spent in the same way. My love for Dorota grew by the day and we became closer as the years past. I was already gaining a reputation as one of the most talented undergraduate surgeons at the university and I couldn't wait to take my love's hand in marriage. As each year passed, I became more and more impatient for this day.

In my third-year winter break I visited Uncle Mathew and Dorota as always, but something was different this time. Instead of being greeted by Dorota, Uncle Mathew answered the door himself. Why was this? I thought. The answer ripped the heart from my chest. Dorota was the guest of a noble family in the town of Cáslav, where she had apparently spent the previous autumn. It was clear that Uncle Mathew wasn't happy about this and said that his daughter had begun to affect the airs and graces of a noblewoman and had started to turn her back on her origins. He saw these noblemen as a bad influence and said that this would be a short phase that she would grow out of. He took my hand as he said this, which reassured me greatly.

The Letter

Returning to my studies for the final year I became more focussed and driven than I had ever been. Nothing would prevent me from passing my degree and returning home to sweep Dorota off her feet. I was comforted by Uncle's last words of encouragement and this helped me focus. As the year progressed, my examinations loomed. However, I was confident that with Dorota's love in my heart I would pass with flying colours and by summer we would marry.

The following Wednesday, three months before my final medical examinations, I received a letter. Recognising the wax postal mark from my hometown, I ripped the letter open with a manic animal energy. The letter was from Uncle.

My dearest Jan,

I hope you are keeping well, and your studies are progressing. I have some urgent news regarding Dorota, the nature of which I cannot discuss in this letter. I ask for you to return to Chrudim as urgently as you possibly can so I can explain the situation. I am sorry I can't be clearer than this. Please hurry.

Kind Regards,
Uncle Mathew

Chrudim

As my carriage sped through the Spring fog towards Chrudim, my mind was racing. What had happened to Dorota? Why was my help needed so urgently? I decided to take a stop just outside the town to clear my head and have a cup of wine at a tavern to calm my nerves. The giant brass sign hanging over the tavern was in the shape of a raven, its long beak arrogantly pointing upwards. It was surprisingly full for such an early hour as I pushed through to the bar. A giant pig's head was inlayed into the wooden beam above it, its face smiling at me mockingly as I ordered my drink. As I drank my first sip, something caught my ear. At first, I thought I had imagined it but again I heard the name. Dorota. Was I going mad?

'What is this talk of Dorota Mydlár, I hear?'

'Dorota Mydlár? Don't you mean Dorota Vanura, the bride of the widowed miller?' The barman said.

'What on earth do you mean, the miller's bride?' I said.

'Where have you been boy? Didn't you hear the news? She is now the proud wife of that old fart down the road, the widowed miller Mr. Vanura.'

'But how could such a sweet virgin marry such an old, wretched man as Vanura?'

'Virgin, I hear you say. It's not what I heard!' The barman loudly retorted as the whole tavern exploded with laughter.

Poor Jan slowly sank, pale faced into a waiting bar stool.

When I visited Uncle, he was a shadow of his formal self. He told me the reason why Dorota had to rush into the marriage was that she was in the family way as a result of one of the noblemen and marrying the old widowed Mr. Vanura was a way for the problem to go away. Poor Uncle's ill health had got the better of him during this time and he had sunk into a deep depression. I tried to console him but in the back of my mind all I could think of was my own loss and sorrow.

The Crime

When I returned to university I had completely lost interest in my studies and was more focussed on the taverns instead. Many a night I spent drowning my sorrows in the various beer halls and inns of Prague and I must have visited every single one. How could such a thing happen? My love had been taken away in such a cruel way by these corrupt, so called noblemen. My sadness was slowly curdling into rage and hatred for these men.

A few months after my return, just a few weeks before my final medical exams, I received another letter. The news from Chrudim become even more strange. Dorota's baby had mysteriously passed away!

Although I was saddened by the news, I couldn't help but feel hopeful that this could be my chance to be reunited with my love once more. But as I read further, my heart sank with disbelief. Dorota, with the help of three witches, had been accused of trying to poison her husband and though he had survived, she had been thrown in the gaol. Poor Dorota would surely die by the hand of the executioner!

My love for Dorota was instantly turned from desperation into inspiration. Action was needed. An action that would change the trajectory of my life path forever - I will free my Dorota from the gaol and I knew exactly how I would do it! I raced to Chrudim with the only thought of rescuing my Dorota. Missing my medical exams would be a small price to pay for her freedom.

The Executioner

It was early evening. As I approached the tall, spike topped gates of the Chrudim city gaol, the guardsman blocked my way. I explained calmly that I was the city doctor on official business, but he laughed in my face with foul smelling breath, the which I had never smelt in my life. 'No doctors needed here, I'm afraid! The only man allowed through these gates is the city executioner.'

With a knowing nod, I offered a purse of coins that I had prepared for this very situation.

'You trying to bribe a public official?' He asked with a threatening scowl. 'Because if you are, I will report you to the mayor and you shall meet a similar fate to those incarcerated within these gates. Now get out before I sound the alarm!'

With that, I ran as far as I could until I reached an isolated part of the city. Breathless, I bent over to try to calm my beating chest. As I regained my composure, the realization of where I had stopped occurred to me as fateful destiny. I had arrived outside the dwelling of none other than the Chrudim executioner. Its looming presence illuminated by one solitary light coming from inside one of the windows. In that split second, I recalled the guardsman's words and hatched the plan of how to enter the gaol to rescue Dorota.

I approached the house and nervously knocked on the door. Instantly, a pack of dogs came growling and barking to the side gate of the property. In the darkness, I could just about see their slavering teeth and black mangled claws scraping from underneath the courtyard fence.

I was relieved when the front door opened and Jirí, the portly town executioner welcomed me inside. As Chrudim was a small town, he immediately recognised me and beckoned me to sit by the fire. I explained the story of my love for Dorota in detail but with the one deceitful addition of why I wanted to enter the gaol to see her. I explained that I wanted to see Dorota punished first-hand for what she had done, and what better way to do this than to work for the executioner.

I offered to work for only food and lodging, and in return Jirí would allow me to witness Dorota's brutal execution. He felt pity upon me and was flattered that a man of such upbringing and professional qualification would want to work for him. He also noted that my anatomical knowledge would be useful for the job at hand, and that wound healing and bone fixing had always been a good way of gaining additional income for an executioner. We celebrated with a strong cup of ale and I was shown to my lodgings. In the morning my training would start. I would have a lot to learn from this master executioner.

The Apprenticeship

Following a hearty breakfast of meat, we got to work. We began with Jirí's basement of horror, where all manner of retched implements were kept. I was gleefully introduced to the tools of his trade; knee splitters; thumbscrews; tongue extractors and ear slicers; the list went on. He described what each one did in gory detail. For example, the Spanish boot, a form of booted leg device was designed to gradually crush the wearer's leg in excruciating pain. The Choking Pear was a wooden mouth shaped block that slowly suffocated the victim, while the Ladder Rack stretched the victim's limbs until they snapped. All were a reminder that the executioner's job was not to merely end life, but also to prolong it in agony if necessary.

Following that ghoulish introduction, Jirí carefully led me through to the sword room. The atmosphere in this space was one of almost monastic calm and silence. The air was cooler, purer. I had sensed this feeling before but couldn't place from when or where. My daydreaming was brought to an abrupt end as Jirí, in a bellowing rasp, began to explain the history of each and every weapon hanging in this sacred space.

The Legend

After detailing the technical capabilities of a few of Jirí's favourite swords, I noticed a strange looking piece hanging on its own on one wall. It was almost as if it was apart from all the other weapons. Its long double handle had an ornate snake-like pattern of which I had never seen before. The base of the weapon had a detailed animal head design; a dragon or lion that I couldn't distinguish in the dim light. At its rounded tip there were three evenly spaced holes in a triangular configuration. However, the most remarkable aspect was its size. It easily had twice the proportions of the other swords on display.

'Ah the Spanish Sword,' Jirí remarked.

'This was used during the Hussite wars when the prisoners were stronger than they are today. The executioner had to grip the sword with both hands in order to get a good purchase. Made of old Spanish steel, nothing is equal to it both in terms of strength and sharpness. The power of the sword was such that the head would come off in one blow, and many a time the head would go spinning into the air much to delight of the jeering crowds.' Jirí's eyes were full of wistful emotion as he recounted this tale.

Slightly disturbed by this, I asked why it was called The Spanish Sword. He told me it had been made in Toledo and showed me the ornate engraving at its hilt.

'There is a legend about this sword well known to all executioners but never mentioned beyond such circles,' Jirí continued. 'I remember that day vividly as if it were yesterday. In 1580 on the morning of Thursday after St. Lucas Day, I was sitting in this very room. I heard an unfamiliar sound. It was a faint ringing or clanging not unlike the sound of distant church bells. I suddenly noticed the sword was moving. It had swung three times against the other swords hanging next to it, creating three clear bell-like chimes. As the climate was cold and autumnal, there was not a window open in the room, so there was no wind to have caused such a thing.'

I sat transfixed by the story as Jirí continued.

'A week later at the exact same time the sword had chimed, The Spanish Sword took the life of a corrupt nobleman, Voderadsky Knight of Hrušov. Due to his social standing, the nobleman was never expected to be executed, but it seemed that justice had been served just this once, justice from the hand of this sword.

Every executioner believes that the executioner's sword has a life of its own. You see those three holes at the tip of the sword? They allow the blood of the executed to enter the weapon and live inside, to become part of it, so to speak. Right now, the holes are open so that means the sword will have another victim soon enough. Only when the holes disappear will the sword rest to never take another life.'

'Twenty years ago, on Christmas day a small boy with his mother entered my residence for medical help. As you well know, the work of an executioner is sometimes that of a wound healer and this boy had a cut to the leg that wouldn't repair itself. While I was bandaging the wound following treatment, a disturbing thing happened. The sword chimed three times. I knew from that day forth that one day the boy would be executed with this sword.

Over the years, I followed the boy's life closely, and sure enough he fell in with a gang of vagrants involved in petty theft. He was arrested on many occasions for such crimes. However, one evening he took part in the robbery of a church. This was sacrilege and he was condemned to death. I beheaded him with this very sword, the same sword that had rung out three times 15 years earlier to announce his impending death. As you can see, the executioner's sword has its own life and memory.'

I began to warm to Jirí as he told me of these stories, and his enthusiasm was infectious. Despite his gruesome profession and his dedication to it, he was a kind, hospitable man who had welcomed me into his home. I began to feel guilty about deceiving him about my real motivations and vowed to repay him in any which way I could.

I sat stunned and now utterly convinced by the power of this weapon. It almost made me forget about my mission to save Dorota. As I slept that night, I had feverish dreams of spinning heads flying over rapturous crowds, ringing bells, and whispering serpent heads.

The next morning when I entered the kitchen, I was met by an atmosphere of frenetic energy and industry. I asked the kitchen lady what was happening. With a broad smile, she informed me that the date for Dorota and the witches to be sentenced to death was to be next week and preparations had already begun. My stomach turned at the news. My plan for her escape had to come sooner than I thought.

Dorota

At breakfast, seven days before the execution of my poor Dorota, I casually asked what preparations were being made at the gaol for the big day. Jirí explained that as the witches were to be burnt, a specially constructed frame had to be designed in the town square. He also said that Dorota would be transferred from the gaol to a new cell nearer the town square, before the day of the execution. This was my chance, I thought. I casually asked which day the transfer would happen and told Jirí that I would like to see Dorota's terrified face as she was moved near to where she was to be beheaded.

'Beheaded?' Jirí asked. 'Oh no, there'll be no beheading this time. The punishment for her crime will be far worse.' My heart sank into the pit of my chest. I hoped that look of horror on my face could have passed as excitement in front if my master.

'She's to be buried alive.' Jirí slurped the last morsel of breakfast into his cavernous mouth and concluded. 'And you are going to do the burying. Don't say I don't look after you boy.' He winked.

I swallowed hard and tried to contain myself as I looked into my breakfast of greasy meats. It took every ounce of will power for me not to vomit all over the table. Nevertheless, this would be my opportunity to save Dorota and I already had a plan.

The day approached for when Dorota was to be moved to her new cell. It was easy for my master to allow me to enter the cell because we had been visiting the execution site daily to prepare the stage for the witches. I told him that I wanted to be alone as she was transferred, and he was more than happy to oblige.

My stomach turned with nausea as I approached the gates of her cell. A guard blocked my way with his bulky body. However, his master beckoned for me to enter and the guard stood aside. Inside was Dorota, her beautiful blonde hair matted to her face, her familiar dress now ragged and stained.

The minute she saw me she cried out my name. Whether she was crying out in hope or shame, I could not distinguish. I whispered carefully in her ear of my plan and showed her the concealed weapon I had stolen from master Jirí's collection. Her tearful eyes fixed mine with a look I had never seen before. It filled me with a strength and inner energy I had never felt before.

The rescue would be sudden. The guards would not suspect such an attack.

At a set time, I had arranged a swift carriage to take us far away from Chrudim, and far away from Dorota's misery and despair!

The Rescue

On the previous visit to the gaol with Jirí, I had noticed a small, low side entrance leading off from the main internal corridor near Dorota's cell. This gated entrance led to a narrow tunnel used to transport coal and opened out to the external courtyard of the building. Before today's visit, I had loosened the lock on its gate using one of master Jiri's tools and hidden a chain inside to restrain the guard.

As the time approached for Dorota to be moved, the guard entered the cell. As Dorota was led through the narrow entrance of her cell door, I made sure I was stood behind the guard as we exited. We walked a few metres down the dank, dimly lit corridor. Just a few feet more was the second to last torch on the left wall. Past the coal scuttle on the right was the entrance to the side alley. Right there I grabbed the guard from behind by his throat. He was so surprised that his weapon fell to the floor and I pushed him down to the entrance of the low gate. He tried to resist, and with shaking hands, I swiftly brandished my knife in the direction of his throat. Taking the chains, I tied the guard to the gate and gagged him with a rag torn from Dorota's gown. I lowered Dorota's head into the corridor and followed after her. Crawling on all fours, we made our way swiftly along its damp coal strewn floor, scraping our skin as we went. A rat the size of which I had never seen before heaved past us with the strength of a small dog. I grabbed Dorota's hand to re-assure her. The light of the courtyard was just in sight and we hurried along towards our freedom.

Jiri

I jumped out of the coal tunnel entrance into the courtyard and helped Dorota down to the ground. With our backs to the wall, we made our way through the large courtyard. But just as we reached the main exit gate, a small phalanx of men came marching from the opposite end of the courtyard towards us. Ducking into a shadowy nook in the fortification wall, I covered Dorota's body with mine. The guards stopped and turned in our direction as if automatically drawn to where we were hiding. As we breathed heavily in the damp air, condensation escaped from our mouths like smoke. Suddenly a loud bell rang out and the men seemed to disperse into set positions in each corner of the courtyard as if alerted to something. Had the incapacitated guard been found already? I could feel Dorota's heart pound against mine as we held on to each other. As the last guard left the courtyard, the bells ceased. We waited.

After a short while it was evident that the guards had been involved in some form of practise manoeuvre. With relief, we looked at each other and set off towards the main gate through the now thickening fog of night. As we ran through the gate, a giant raven perching on one of the parapets screamed out and turned its ugly head around repeatedly as if to announce our escape. More ravens flew in. Soon his feathered cohort was joining in with a hideously shrill chorus of disapproval. There must have been over one hundred ugly birds screaming down at us from the one side of the castle rooftop. We ran in the direction of the nearest wooded area we could see. As if sensing our urgency, the ravens immediately pealed upwards and coursed down upon us. It was as if the castle was disintegrating upwards into the air piece by piece. The already darkening sky became pitch black as we ran and ran until we could run no more.

The tavern I had stopped off at on the way to Chrudim that fateful time before, was the place we would meet and sure enough the coach was there. Breathless and thirsty I went ahead to find some water for us, and I told Dorota to hide out of site. The horses were feeding in preparation for the long journey, but the coachman was not present. I carefully stepped past the horses and walked around the coach. Something wasn't right. I swiftly jumped up and entered the vehicle. Inside, with his arms crossed, Jirí was sitting looking at me with contempt and disappointment. I recoiled in shock stepping backwards out of the coach. I would have fallen to the ground if I hadn't been blocked by the bulk of one of Jirí's men. Jirí jumped down from the carriage with a menacing thump and nodded to the tavern.

'Time for a drink, don't you think.'

It seemed an inappropriate time to celebrate, but I was in no position to argue.

The Tavern

There were not many drinkers inside the tavern. However, as always, Jirí gesticulated towards the bar for me to buy the ales as he skulked over to a dark corner; it was customary for an executioner to drink separately from the rest of the patrons and in some taverns an area was specially designated for them.

I brought the ales over to the table and we sat opposite each other in silence.

'Next time if you steal one of my weapons, make sure it isn't one of my best ones.' He gestured with a nod and a smile to my waist. Nervously I unstrapped the weapon and handed it over like a child who had stolen an apple from a farmer. I asked him what he had done with Dorota.

'She's safe now boy, don't you worry about her.'

Jirí took a big slurp of ale and wiped his greasy beard down.

My heart jumped at the thought that Jirí was a good man. We had become friends over the months of my training, and I felt him to be good man. A noble man. Maybe he could find it in his heart to be understanding.

But as he continued talking, he began looking out of the window at nothing in particular. This unnerved me greatly.

'Now Jan. I have a problem. We have a problem. I'm proud of what I do for this parish. It's the only thing I am truly good at, you see. I'm part of the community. People rely on me. Look up to me.'

This was not sounding good.

'One of my employees, namely you, has helped a convicted prisoner to escape. This just doesn't look good.'

I nodded and looked down at my hands in shame.

'I trusted you Jan. I helped you and this is what you do to me?'

I was shocked to see tears in his eyes. A nervous silence filled the air.

'But there is a way we can resolve the situation. A way you can fix my...*our*, problem.'

With that he reached into a large sack he had beside him and Jirí threw the burial shovel down onto the table.

'If you bury this whore in front of the good people of Chrudim next week, all will be good. If you don't, you and I will surely be the ones hanging from those gallows instead. It's a simple choice and I strongly recommend that you make the right one.'

xxv | Headcase

I stared straight ahead. I looked but I could not see. It was as if Jirí was invisible. I told him I would not do such a thing. I could not. With a swipe of my hand I knocked the shovel to the hard stone floor with crash.

'This is your last chance Jan.'

I continued to stare ahead as if in a witch's trance. I had made up my mind.

Jirí nodded over to one of his men standing by the tavern entrance.

'Let's go for a nice walk, shall we.'

He picked up the shovel and continued to talk as we left the tavern.

'You know Jan, there are many forms of loyalty in this world. Loyalty to your country. To your Parish. Loyalty to your master.'

With this last word. His voice cracked with emotion.

'But you know the most important loyalty of all?'
'Family.'

With that, Jirí's guard pulled back the covering at the rear of the carriage to reveal a frail and shaking Uncle Mathew. He had been bound and gagged.

'Now, the choice is simpler for you. Either you bury that whore next week or I will bury her father here tonight.'

With his flamed torch, he gestured over to a freshly dug hole in the forest floor just a few metres from the coach.

'So, what is it to be?'

And so, on that night in 1586 the light was altered. It was not the light of a candle gently illuminating a room, but of one being violently extinguished; an explosion in reverse containing everything that had been good before this night. University was gone. The summer days with Uncle Mathew. Dorota. Everything fell away with a sickening backward rush. Jan almost felt a sense of cold relief that all was lost. No more fighting. No more good. No more bad. From this day forth, Jan Mydlár was reborn.

Chapter 1
THE SHOP

The warrens of tourist shops on Nerudova Street were starting to open for the day. Svetlana yawned as she pulled up the heavy metal shutter covering her small gift shop. She was proud of the business she had built up. It was considered the go-to destination for all things ghoulish and kitsch in the city; Trump and Putin masks jostled for space with gorilla suits and naughty nurse outfits. Everything one would need for a stag or hen weekend was there.

The horror masks were the real draw though, and they took pride of place in a long horizontal line above the front desk of the shop that faced onto the street.

However, something was different this morning. Svetlana couldn't exactly place it. An almost imperceptible change. Air pressure? temperature? something. She looked up and shook her head. Probably too many Becherovkas last night. Hangovers were becoming more and more intolerable, and she put the feeling of unease down to the fact she had drunk far too much the previous night.

She wiped a bead of sweat from her brow and decided to press on with her day.

Then. As she looked up again, she noticed what was different about the shop.

One. Two. Three. Four. Five... Six?
Putin. Trump. Obama. Gates. Gorilla and...

Her hangover was brought to an abrupt cold jolt as a dollop of blood plopped onto a giant inflatable cock sitting on the front desk.

As she looked up, she noticed a grotesque addition to the mask selection; a severed head had been placed, last in line. She dropped her large bunch of shop keys onto the hard flagstone floor and rushed out of the door in panic as a black Prius glided up the road. It narrowly missed her as she fumbled for her phone to call the police.

Chapter 2
THE INVESTIGATION

Chief Inspector, Tomáš Novák arrived at the novelty shop on Nerudova Street.

Svetlana was smoking her third cigarette as she nervously sipped from a Starbucks coffee cup. The coffee was cold now, but she didn't notice.

The focus of Novák's investigation was a question. The shop had been locked when Svetlana arrived but how was the head already inside the shop? The investigation's focus had to be who had access to the shop. A list was drawn up of family members, employees and the cleaning company Svetlana used.

As forensics went about its business, Novák stared at the decapitated head. There was something puzzling about the scene (other than the fact it was a severed head amongst a selection of novelty masks). A certain imbalance in air pressure, something familiar perhaps.

Three days later, forensics emailed the main report. As Novák scanned the document, two details jumped out at him. The first was that the victim had a tattoo of a small cross behind the ear. Looking at the report photos, he noticed that the cross was not a typical Christian design, but instead had equal proportions, very much like the cross you would see on a keyboard or calculator. The cross was stubbier and compact too. The other notable detail was that the incision on the neck was thought to have been made in one blow and not by a heavy object like an axe, but by a narrower weapon like a sword or a large knife. This last detail was the most useful; it would take a very strong blow to remove a head with such a weapon, requiring a fair amount of skill and accuracy. Novák called the lead forensic to confirm this important detail as it seemed too implausible. Why would someone go to the trouble of committing such a crime in this way? None of it made sense. Then again, leaving a head in a joke shop didn't make much sense either.

The first investigative interview was scheduled for 12 midday with the owner of the business, a Svetlana Beránková. The interview room was set up with a digital recorder and an assistant police investigator already seated opposite the interviewee. Svetlana looked drawn and nervous. Based on the report, there had been no clear connection between her and the victim but nevertheless this line of questioning was the first to get out of the way. She went on to explain that she had opened the shop that morning at exactly the same time she did every morning. She didn't seem to have any enemies who wanted to disrupt her life in any way and no other staff members had access to the shop; she ran a tight ship on narrow margins and liked the way she could fully control the management of the place. As Novák suspected, she didn't seem directly connected to the murder but there was still the glaring question of access. Svetlana was asked about the cleaning company she used. They did have access to the shop and the weekly cleaning day was on Sunday, the day before the murder. In addition, she had recently started to use a new company. This was promising. After he had concluded the interview, Nokák asked the assistant to follow up on the cleaning company contact details and to get a meeting ASAP.

Chapter 3
FROSTY JACKS - BREAKFAST OF CHAMPIONS

Novák woke at 7:30 am to the familiar sound of construction in his street. The municipality had recently started to re-enforce the foundations of his apartment, resulting in the daily toing and froing of construction workers and heavy vehicles. The hammering of metal on stone synchronised with the mild pounding in his head from his hangover. The night before he had been celebrating his daughter's birthday with a small group of her friends. Considering he had forgotten Tereza's birthday yesterday morning, it was a good night. At least he thought it was a good night. Was it a good night? Vague memories of an encounter in a toilet with one of her daughter's girlfriends were confirming that it had been a good night for him but possibly not for his daughter. Tereza tolerated her father's behaviour in the way a parent tolerated the way a two year old breaks things around the house. Tomáš knew this, and not unlike a satanic toddler, took full advantage of this dynamic.

Breakfast time. One-part Cornflakes, one-part milk, one-part Jack Daniels. Breakfast time always meant Frosty Jack time. Novák was preparing for a particularly bad day. Facing the press wasn't his forté and this morning was going to be the shit storm of all press meetings. As Novák had risen through the ranks, his role increasingly appeared to be more about managing reality, reality of the investigation versus reality of the media. Bearing in mind a severed head had been found in a shop, this was not going to be easy to spin. Novák was going to be pulled in every direction by various Prague "stakeholders". Everyone had their own agenda, from the Ministry of Tourism through to the media outlets with their political affiliations.

As the press scrum gathered in the pelting rain, Novák pushed out of the glass doors to the paved area in front of the Městská Policie Headquarters.

Novák pointed at one of the reporters.

The first question rang out from a reporter from Blesk Newspaper.

'Is it true the severed head might be terrorist related?'

'We still don't know the motivation behind the killing, and we will be following all leads to find who did this.' Tomáš replied.

'Thank you. Andrej Svoboda from Mladá Fronta. Could the recent rise in immigrants be the reason for more and more violence in the city?'

'We have no reason to believe immigration is anything to do with this or any other crime like this. Like I said, we will be following all avenues but at this time, we have no new information.'

'Yes you' Novák pointed to the next reporter.

'Alice Černý, from Právo. The Czech-Moravian Confederation has said that the treatment of shop workers might be to blame for the murder and that this could have been a suicide.'

'No, it's not possible to cut your own head off as far as we know.' Novák countered placidly.

'Any information leading to the killer can be sent to the Městská Policie Headquarters email address, press inquiries can be sent to our press relations department. All contact details are on the Městská Policie Headquarters website. Now if there are no more questions, I'll hand you over to our head investigator.' That was Novák's cue to escape and start the real work.

Chapter 4
THE HOTEL ROOM

It was mid-morning. Darius Marcus sauntered over in his hotel slippers to the brightly lit window of his suite at The Alchymist Grand Hotel in Prague.

His white fluffy dressing gown felt good. He let out a long fart. Despite its length, it was almost inaudible. It was the fart of a man with little on his mind. It eased out of its own volition, uninhibited by stress, urgency or even purpose.

But this morning felt different. Darius sensed something he hadn't felt in years. It was so unfamiliar he didn't even know what it was. Fear? Nah.

Out of the corner of his left eye he noticed a movement. In a split second he turned to look. The room was decorated in a faux-medieval style, replete with a regal four poster bed, draped in Italianate fabrics. Two giant axes sat over the 17th Century style fireplace in a criss-cross fashion. He could have sworn that they were moving, not much, just a gentle wobble. But the moment he stared at them, they stopped. What the fuck. Darius said 'bollocks' under his breath and laughed to himself.

He had been in the city to personally oversee the latest shipment, the truck was to be delivered to the port in Holland and Prague was a transit point. Russian, Chinese, Slovaks mainly. One had died of hypothermia but there was always bloody something. He would have to offer a discount to the end buyer but nothing insurmountable.

Chapter 5
THE MEETING

Novák had been called to a crisis meeting at the headquarters of the Ministry of Public affairs. Since the head had been discovered the whole of Prague was in panic mode. However absurd it seemed, rumours about a terrorist invasion were spreading like wildfire and it was felt that something had to be done to dampen the media coverage while an investigation took place.

As he entered the glass and steel office, Novák was greeted by The Minster of The Interior, The Ministry of Prague Tourism, The Government's communications team and a bald, skeletal man he didn't recognise. Each participant introduced themselves in an orderly clockwise fashion around the dark wooden conference table. Coffee was poured and documents were distributed.

After a briefing by The Minster of The Interior and a plea from the head of The Minister of Prague Tourism to desperately do something about the depleted tourist numbers, the tall skinny man who had introduced himself as Jakub Smutny, stood up to present his solutions to the crisis. Novák had come across these people before, PR experts often called upon when the normal avenues of crisis management were exhausted. Novák didn't really want to be there. However, he gave Smutny the benefit of the doubt as he started the presentation.

'Minister, thank you for inviting me here during this difficult time. People are scared. Tourism is down. People are afraid to go out at night and Prague has never seen anything like it in recent memory. Although this is a grave situation, we have an opportunity to fix this. I have always said that a crisis is an opportunity in disguise, and this is a crisis like no other.' The others present looked at each other with quizzical faces, not knowing what to expect next.

'We are at a crossroads in mass human communication. There has never been less trust in democratic institutions. We now have the opportunity to control what people think and what we don't want them to think. We have the tools to be able to control the information flow. To release it. Steer it. Stop it. Start it. Even CHANGE it.

If we can prove that all information is false, we can feed the public anything we want. The post-truth world is upon us and we should take full advantage of this mistrust in supposedly official information.'

'Ladies and gentlemen, let me introduce OPERATION FAKE HEAD!' On cue, Smutny's young assistant stood up and started clapping. The silence in the room was deafening and the assistant promptly sat down, as more confused faces looked around the room for something to hold on to.

A cough punctuated the constipated silence.

'Did you just say FAKEHEAD?' The Minister of The Interior said.

'Yes, FAKEHEAD, it has a certain ring to it, don't you think?' Smutny said in a self-congratulatory way.

Novák started looking at his phone messages.

'What does it exactly mean, FAKEHEAD?' The Minister of Prague Tourism, chimed in.

Now everyone was murmuring amongst themselves. All you could hear was FAKEHEAD this, FAKEHEAD that. It sounded like a mental hospital at breaktime.

'Please, please.' Smutny interrupted. 'If you just let me explain.'

A shushing sound ended the hubbub of voices.
And with that, Smutny clicked the overhead remote to reveal a grotesque severed head on the screen. The room gasped in horror.

'This was a decapitated head recovered from a battle ground in Basra in Iraq.'

'While this.' He clicked the remote again.

'Is a head created by our FX Prosthesis Team.'

The projector displayed an identical looking head. The two were virtually indistinguishable.

'Say hi to Bob.' "Hi Bob". Smutny gave a wave with a giggle.

'Basra. Bob. Basra. Bob.' As he flicked between the two photographs on the projector.

'Now, as you know, we have a head problem in Prague. We also have a tourist problem. What better way to encourage the tourists back than to simply say that the heads are fake? By planting Bob in a prominent tourist spot and reporting on it, we have the perfect way to do that. We change the conversation. We control the information. We increase the tourism.'

'I like to call this C.C.I - Change, Control, Increase.'

The room fell silent.

'What about the previous murder that was real?' Novák asked.

'Oh, that'll be forgotten about soon enough, it's just a case of making a bigger noise about the one that isn't real, to drown out the coverage about the one that is.' Smutny countered.

'This is all well and good Mr. Smutny but what about the investigation.' The Minster of The Interior asked.

'What investigation?' Smutny asked.

'The real murder of a real dead person' Novák said, raising his voice.

'Oh yes, of course. Well, that will be taken care of by you Mr. Novák. No?' Smutny responded curtly with a wave of his hand in Novák's direction.

'So, you are expecting me to conduct a proper police investigation while a fake head is found in... where did you say, exactly?' He pointed to the document handout. '... a public place to maximise the impact of the media coverage. Am I supposed to be a fake detective and investigate this fake head as well?'.

'No, not this fake head. Mr. Novák, these...'

Smutny clicked the projector to reveal the final slide of his presentation. One image displaying a rogue's gallery of fake heads. There must have been over 30 of them staring out at the projected image filling the room.

Chapter 6
THE AUCTION

Darius Marcus folded the lavish auction brochure under his arm as the chauffeur opened the door of the waiting limousine outside the hotel. He was on the way to an auction of "Fine and rare things" just outside the city. He had become an avid collector over the years and this particular auction had caught his eye. Weapons were a favourite of his, and this event promised to be an opportunity to expand his collection. It was not unusual for him to spend over $100,000 on one item at an event like this and he was looking forward to it.

Walking through the main entrance hall of the auction house, Darius noticed something that unnerved him; two axes situated above one of the entrances to the main auction hall. Strange that he hadn't seen these on previous trips. He swerved deftly through the adjacent entrance without hanging axes, the way you would avoid walking under a ladder in the street. As the other guests were beginning to fill up the substantial auction hall inside, he decided to take a walk around. With a perfectly manicured lawn, the outside area was a 100 sq. foot inner courtyard appointed with classical sculptures and giant brass and pewter animal figures; artfully placed ornamental planters complimented the overhanging branches of a huge weeping willow as a water feature bubbled away in the background.

The familiar voice of Mario, the Italian curator of the event, entered the courtyard. With bright veneered teeth bared, he came striding up to Darius and strongly shook his hand. Darius was a valued patron of these events and received many "perks" as a result; Mario introduced him to two of his friends, Alice and Bibiana both in possession of unfeasibly pneumatic breasts. They would be sent to his hotel suite that evening free of charge this time. A waiter appeared and Champagne was poured.

Darius read the auction catalogue as he sipped his Champagne. All the items for sale were displayed with beautiful full colour photographs detailing their provenance, specification and starting price. There was an ornate Tabar war axe from 18th Century Persia ($890), an English Civil War Burgonet Helmet (starting at $4,400), an English Military Hanger by Horns Clemens Solingen from 1586-1617 ($3,800). He could hardly contain himself. One thing really caught his eye though. What looked like a 17th Century double handed sword had been withdrawn from sale. Its ornamental handle with a snake pattern was something he had never seen before. What was also strange was that for its age (Circa Late 1500s), it was in perfect condition. Darius had never seen such a thing. He had to have it. He needed it.

The auction went well. At the Champagne reception, after bidding successfully for an object called a Spanish Boot (a snip at just shy of $3,000) and a dagger ($400), both from 17th Century Bohemia, Darius approached Mario about the withdrawn executioner's sword.

'Oh that. Bit of a sore point actually.' Mario replied with his baritone Italian accent.

'Very amusing', Darius countered.

'No seriously, it has been a nightmare Darius, I can't tell you. Just a few days after this month's auction was set up, I had a burglary. The strange thing was, there was no break-in and the only thing stolen was that one item.

'Go on.' Darius said.

'I reported it to the Police, but I haven't heard any news yet. Whoever stole it knew what they were looking for though. That thing was rare and very old. Most examples have fallen into disrepair or been lost and there are a lot of fakes out there, but I can assure you this one was the real deal. It was worth around $20,000 – I'd have given it to you for $35,000'. Mario joked with a slap to his back.

'Mario, go fuck yourself.'

'I don't have to, the insurance company already did.'

'I haven't heard anything from the police, and it happened months ago. If you want to get in touch with them, I can give you the guy's number.'

With that, Mario searched through his wallet for the card he was given by the investigator, fished it out and handed it over.

It would seem this trip was going to be more interesting than Darius thought, as he got into the waiting limousine. So, straight to the hotel for a shower and to wait for his other treasures; Alice and Bibiana would be arriving at 9pm.

Chapter 7
BLACK EYE

The following morning, Darius woke to the sound of knocking on the door of his hotel suite. It was that gentle knocking that only 5-star hotels knew how to do. He wondered if there was a course they did for that at Hotel School. Sitting up, he noticed a pain under his right eye. Just a dull ache but still sore, nevertheless. The bedroom was a chaotic battlefield of bottles, broken glasses, silver service plates and full ashtrays. There was a red stiletto stuck into the top of a giant untouched tower of profiteroles. The music system was still belting out a local EDM radio station. Darius was amazed he could have slept through it. Reaching over, he switched the music off before opening the door to the smiling young face of one of the concierge staff. They had been trying to call his room all morning. Looking past Darius at the room's state, the baby-faced concierge passed a note to Darius and asked if there was anything else he needed. Darius declined the offer, thanked him and closed the door. Yawning, he entered the large heavily mirrored bathroom of his suite and was shocked to discover he had the makings of a black eye; his right eyelid was a puce, yellowish colour and there was a faint brown discolouration above his cheek.

As he stepped into the shower, the previous evening's shenanigans unfolded like pages of an animated flicker book. Not again, he thought. Although he liked girls with enormous fake breasts, there was always the risk of injury when they swung in one's face and believe it or not, this wasn't the first time it had happened. Note to self: BE MORE CAREFUL WITH THE SILICON. He stepped out of the shower and picked up the slip of paper the concierge had delivered: Call Marius re sword +420 734 311 808.

Getting dressed, Darius dialed the number and got through to Mario's PA. The line clicked through to silence. Mario's booming voice then came on the line.

'Hey, how is my favourite collector?'

'Sore head, sore eye, but other than that fine and dandy, you called earlier.'

'Yes, yes. It appears there is more information about your missing sword Darius. According to the police it is thought to be still in the country. A few weeks ago, they tracked it down to an independent online auction site with an IP address based just east of Prague in a place called Chrudim. The bad news is the lead investigator won't talk to anyone about this matter other than me for some reason, so good luck with getting any information out of him. By the way how were the girls?'

'Thanks Mario. The girls were splendid.'

'Don't say I don't look after you, Darius.'

'Yeah. Yeah, whatever.'

Darius hung up the phone.

So, the hunt was on and now he knew just where to start; the sprat to catch the mackerel.

As he walked out of the revolving doors of the hotel entrance, the Ducati was waiting for him and Darius tipped the valet. Darius started up the engine and slowly glided away from the hotel to the east of the city towards Chrudim.

Chapter 8
THE VISITOR CENTRE

Another 6am start. The cleaner unlocked the large glass front door of the visitor centre on The Old Town Square. Blinking at his watch, he realised he would have time for a coffee before performing all of his morning duties. He made his way through the main foyer with its arched brickwork hallway towards the staff kitchen. Crouching down to open the refrigerator, he sniffed the milk carton. As he stood to reach for the kettle on the countertop, he heard an unusual sound for this time in the day; rock music, combined with an electric whirring sound. Bloody stag weekends he thought. Every week, gangs of drunk tourists invaded Prague with the pure intention of partying, and every morning, the evidence of the previous night's revelries were to be found in all the surrounding streets; used condoms, broken bottles, vomit, cigarette butts. But the latest 'trend' was to rent Segways and drive them like a maniac in circles around The Old Town Square. The whirring sound he heard was a Segway electric motor turning over. Making his way towards the sound coming from the side of the visitor centre, he could just make out a shape between the mosaic of event posters stuck to the inside of the windowed museum foyer. It seemed as if one of these idiots was banging the window whilst sitting on the Segway. He was a skinny little fucker too. Probably a junky who had stolen one of the vehicles and was now nodding off against the window. He vigorously unstuck the largest of the posters to tell the idiot to piss off through the window.

But there was a reason the headbanger was skinny. He had no body. The Segway's engine was still turning over but had been trapped between a rubbish bin and the visitor centre's window. A dismembered head had been stuck on to the handlebars of the Segway and was comically swinging back and forth in perfect time, as if head banging to the AC/DC that was playing from a small MP3 speaker attached to it. He fell back head over heels, his heart pounding in his chest like a road drill.

Chapter 9
OLD TOWN SQUARE INVESTIGATION

On this occasion the police were not caught off guard and a cordon had been erected rapidly and the cleaner detained so the media couldn't report on it easily. Novák hastily pulled on his coat and headed for The Old Town Square.

Pushing through the now crowded square Novák made his way through the police tape over to the tent covering the crime scene. Eliška Černý, the lead forensic was there, as well as members of Novák's own team. Some of them were making tasteless jokes and seemed almost happy that this had happened. Although Prague had its own problems with various forms of vice, everything they usually investigated was very much below the surface of the city's chocolate-box veneer. They had never seen anything like this in their lifetime and they were clearly excited about it.

The Segway's engine had been switched off and was now propped against the visitor centre. The head was still attached to the vehicle and the mouth had the appearance of a grotesque smile as it leaned heavily on the window. Novák's phone rang yet another time, the call that he had been dreading. It was now decided by the powers that be, that Smutny's misinformation campaign was to be put into action and he was summoned to Police HQ for a briefing.

Chapter 10
OPERATION FAKE HEAD

That afternoon, a meeting chaired by Smutny and just three undercover police had gathered. Needless to say, an iron wall of secrecy was to be placed around the operation and the plant was to be implemented with military precision. There was a popular bowling alley called Bowling Celnice in the centre of the city. This would give as much exposure as possible to the discovery of the head whilst allowing the team to control the placement. The owners of the business had been told that essential maintenance had to be done on the foundations of the bowling alley but would not disrupt the business in any way, as the work would take place on a Sunday. To add to the "authenticity of the optics", Novák had been ordered to be present after the head was discovered but was promised that he could concentrate on the real investigation after the bowling alley operation and he had no obligation to be involved other than this one time. Novák agreed begrudgingly, with the crumb of comfort that he didn't need to waste more time than was necessary and that he was at least "permitted" to do his actual job.

Anyway, Novák had more pressing business today than to worry about these trivialities. He had a meeting out of the city to investigate the theft of an expensive antique sword. The case was a few months old, but Novák couldn't help thinking that there could be a possible link with the shop murder because of the timing. The auction company had a disconnected line which had raised more suspicion. However absurd it seemed, Prague had its fair share of misfits, medieval history nuts, goth dungeon sex parties and cult killings over the years for it to be worth at least a follow up. So far there had been no obvious motives for the killing. The missing person's bulletin came up with nothing related to the age of the victim who had been a 30-year-old male. DNA tests showed that he was of Czech/Hungarian descent but other than the cross tattoo, there was nothing substantial to follow up. The cleaning company that had access to the shop the night before the murder had come up with more dead ends. Anyway, Novák could do with a long drive to clear his head and think. He was under a lot of pressure now there had been another murder and this attempt to cover the murders by Smutny was only adding to the feeling that his investigation was going nowhere.

Chapter 11
THE CHRUDIM INVESTIGATION

The engine on Darius' Ducati burbled as it pulled into Chrudim. With an ornate fountain in the centre of the cobbled Ressel Square and surrounded by pastel-coloured houses dating back to the 17th Century, it was a pleasant enough town, he thought. A farmer's market was being set up and the market workers were busy assembling stalls and displaying their wares before it opened, despite the overcast weather. Darius parked up the Ducati to the side of the square and entered a small cafe. Ordering a double espresso, he sat at one of the tables by the window and pulled out his phone. The local news was still covering the story about a possible murder in Prague involving a dismembered head in a shop. Very nasty indeed, Darius thought. As he scrolled down the page, he zoomed in on the photo of the policeman at the scene with the caption detailing his name. He took out the card Mario had given him and checked. It was the same investigator, Tomáš Novák. The picture was blurry, but it gave Darius at least a rough idea of how he looked; tall, dark hair that was slightly receding in a swept-back widow's peak, dark raincoat, white shirt. He reminded him of someone but couldn't quite work out who. Sipping his coffee, he took in the sights of Chrudim through the large picture window of the cafe. People had started to arrive at the market, and cars were beginning to fill up the spaces around the market square. Outside the cafe, a little girl carrying a doll walked past with her mother, the doll's head was dangling precariously from its body. She waved the doll at Darius and the head bobbed about grotesquely as the little girl giggled through the window at him. Looking past her, Darius noticed a jet black Škoda saloon with heavily tinted windows slowing to a stop at the left corner of the square. It seemed out of place amongst the hum drum family cars and market trader vans in the square. Darius sipped the last of his coffee and pulled out a 5 Euro note. Walking across the square, he could just make out the driver exiting the vehicle. It couldn't be. What was Nicolas Cage doing in Chrudim? Maybe he was here on holiday, it was a possibility. Hats off to his surgeon, Mr. Cage was looking very good for his age. He'd lost a few pounds too. He held up his phone to compare the image of the policeman with the man he saw here. They seemed to match. Confused but determined to follow his instinct about what he assumed was as unmarked police car, he carefully pursued Mr. Cage at a safe distance.

On his phone, Novák checked the details of the physical address linked to the IP. The name of the auction company was Dorota Auctions. Walking up

Bretislavova Street, the heavens started to open. Pulling the collar of his raincoat up around his neck Novák followed the curving cobbled road to somewhere called Sims Burger Bistro. The auction address was behind here according to Google maps. As he passed the window display of the Museum of Puppets, he reached a clothing shop called Milano Moda and noticed something out of the corner of his eye. Someone was following him. He stopped, turned a full 180 degrees and looked back down the curvy lane. He could just make out a middle-aged Japanese lady wearing an umbrella hat filming him through the rain. Novák was used to people mistaking him for Nicolas Cage, and living in a country with so many tourists made this problem even more acute. It made it hard to remain incognito when he was investigating a case, but he had learnt to rise above it over the years.

At the opening of Bretislavova Street, Darius Marcus stopped and noticed a small lady wearing what looked like an umbrella on her head, intently filming something about 10 metres ahead of her. Following her line of sight, he saw that she was filming a man walking up the street. The man turned suddenly. It was Nicolas Cage. Instinctively, Darius moved his head to the right and found himself looking into the dead eyes of a puppet in the window of some folk museum. Standing still, he slowly curved his head left to see if he had been spotted. Nicolas Cage had moved on up the road.

The neon sign of Sims Burger Bistro was an incongruous sight amongst the quaint little shops and alleys. Moving to the side of the restaurant, Novák noticed a broken metal gate that led to some out-buildings across a small car park. Not exactly a salubrious address for an auction company. There was a long grey barn-like structure stretching the length of the small car park with a metal staircase leading up to a small door. A group of guard dogs incarcerated inside an enclosure started growling and scraping at the underneath of the fence that kept them in. By now the rain was pelting down in huge globules as Novák approached the barn.

As Darius followed him further up the lane, he noticed that Cage had stopped by a restaurant with a neon sign and moved into the side alley of the restaurant. Now Darius was certain he wasn't following Nicolas Cage but Tomáš Novák; why the hell would Nicolas Cage be scrabbling about behind a Chrudim burger restaurant in the pissing rain. On second thoughts maybe it was Nicolas Cage. As he peeked in for a closer look, a gang of massive dogs started barking manically at him from behind a fence, the chains of the fence rattling in unison as each bark rang out. Darius recoiled, slipped and almost fell over.

As Novák ascended the side of the barn, the rain was making clanging musical notes of varying pitches on the metal staircase. By now the light was getting bad and he pulled out his Maglite. The door was locked from the outside with a padlock, but it didn't take him long to smash it off with the butt of his heavy-duty torch. Removing his shoes, carefully placing them upright by the door and donning surgical gloves he entered. As he pointed his torch straight into the room, he was immediately confronted by a grinning face at waist height. Moving carefully closer, it appeared to be a life-size puppet head, similar to those used in Czech puppet theatres all over the country. The light switch was not working so he cast his torch around the rest of the room. The long space was a small office of sorts with a long desk on one side of the narrow 8-metre-wide barn. The ceiling was low and felt oppressive and sad, with a sagging roof and mould on the thin and wrinkled carpeting. The smell of the room was like a cross between wet crisps and mildew. To the far end to the right was an internal door. He pulled to open it, but it was tight shut. The door frame looked like it was made of re-enforced steel, the lock had a numbered keypad. Suddenly, the dogs outside started barking again. He switched off his torch with a click.

The torch light that Darius could see coming from the window in the barn suddenly went out. It wouldn't be worth going further, now he knew where the auction was operating from and decided to hang back and run inside Sims Burger Bistro to think what his next move would be.

As Novák only had a provisional search warrant, he wasn't able to break into the internal office door today, so he decided to search for anything useful in the main office area. It was completely empty except for a wireless router, its shape in the low light like a giant insect head with two vertical horns either side of it and two beady red lights for eyes. Pulling away the desk from the wall he heard something drop to the floor with a dull thump. Placing his torch on the floor he reached at the back of the desk and pulled out a small novel sized book. The insect router and the shadow of the puppet head across the wall made the place look like the backdrop to some nightmarish Czech pantomime. He placed the book carefully into an evidence bag, sealed it and cast his torch wider around the room. On the opposite wall, the light picked out a faint rectangular white shape where there had been a poster or notice of some sort, the area beyond its own area, dirty with dust. He carefully took a fingerprint tape to the dust to the right and to the left of the white area and pealed it away from the wall then did the same with the light switch, the router and the surface areas of the desk. He stepped back to observe the scene as closely as he could. The first thing that struck him was the incongruously messy state of the office compared to the masterly way the sword had been stolen from the auctioneers; the same perpetrator who had stolen a rare antique undetected would never have left a veritable treasure trove of evidence behind in this way. Picking up the puppet head as carefully as he could, Novák left the scene satisfied that nothing more could be gleaned from the scene at this time. It was time to interview the owners of the Sims Burger Bistro to see if anything shook out there.

Sims Burger Bistro was an odd mash-up of Gothic castle chic and urban white minimalism. Its medieval stone arched walls were combined with white wooden wall panels and deep red floors making it both homely and strangely threatening at the same time. The tiny restaurant was empty except for Darius sitting at one of the tables staring sadly into his burger. He was woken from his melancholic burger trance by Novák entering the restaurant. Darius pulled out his phone and pretended to be speaking to someone.

Novák showed his police ID to the waiter and asked if anyone knew anything about the tenant of the barn. The waiter walked to the back of the restaurant and returned with the manager. A short middle-aged man with a giant head of curly hair gestured to sit at one of the tables. Due to the restaurant's small size, the table was uncomfortably close to where Darius was sitting. He could more or less hear everything they were talking about. Unfortunately for Darius, Novák could also probably work out that he wasn't really on the phone. Taking a chance, he put the phone down and tried to act normally and bit into his burger. It was surprisingly good. As he chewed away, the questions and answers came.

'How long have you had this business?' Novák asked.

'Two years, approximately.'

'Who owns the building behind you?'

'The freeholders own this whole complex, including the restaurant.'

'Name, please.'

'Masvák Holding.'

'Who usually rents the barn at the back, the one with the metal stairs?', as he points over his shoulder with his pen.

'I don't really know. Our timings don't really match, so we rarely see each other, and he used to keep himself to himself, if you know what I mean.'

'What do you mean used to?'

'We haven't seen him for a few months now. Hey Jerry', he shouted back to the waiter

'It's been about two months since we saw him, right?'

'Who?'

'What do you mean who, the barn guy', he gesticulated to the back of the restaurant.

'Oh yeah, around two to three months, around that', the waiter replied as he stacked drinks in the refrigerator.

'Did you notice anything unusual about him?'

'Not really, hey do I know you? You look really familiar.'

'I'm not him', Novák replied impatiently.

'Who?'

'Never mind. So, can you describe the man who was using the office.'

The manager scratched his dark curly hair.

'Er, middle aged, tall, maybe about 6.2. Oh, he likes his hats. He was always wearing one of those old-style ones, like from the 1940s.'

'Trilby.'

'No, my name's Toby.'

'The hat.'

'Oh yeah, sorry a trilby that's right', kind of British or Frank Sinatra type look. Cool yeah.'

'Anything else?'

'He brought a suitcase a couple of times, like he was going on holiday or something.'

'We called him the holiday guy for a while', he said leaning his chair back.

'Yeah, the holiday guy, the waiter added, laughing.'

Novák took their names and left a card with the manager. It was at that point that he looked up directly at Darius eating his hamburger in the corner of the restaurant.

Staring into space, Darius swallowed the mouthful of meat in one nervous gulp.

Novák stood. Paused in front of Darius and stared at him.

Time froze into two long seconds, his phone rang, he checked the screen and left the restaurant.

Darius breathed out in relief and put down his burger and typed into Google "sword for sale Chrudim" and came up with surprisingly large number of page results. Selecting the images tab produced a page of swords of varying quality and interest. Then he spotted it; the unmistakable handle with its snake design jumped off the page. He clicked through to a site called Dorota.cz. The photo was more detailed than the one from Mario's sales brochure. You could see the base of the handle with a serpent head; the words Toledo were clearly visible near to the hilt. One strange thing stood out to him were the three holes near the tip in a triangular pattern. They seemed to be drilled all the way through to the other side.

Before driving back to Prague Novák checked the Dorota.cz page. According to the bid history there had been five offers over the last two hours already. If the premises were abandoned, how come the auction was still taking place? He made a call through to police HQ for a fix on the IP again and put in a request for a full search of the office.

As he was driving back to Prague Novák got a call from his daughter Tereza, he picked up on the car's Bluetooth speaker.

'Hey peanut.'

'Dad, I'm 22 years old.'

'I know, peanut.'

'OK, you can stop now. I've got some good news.'

'I like good news.'

'They want me to do a speech at an event at the film school and I want you to come.' She said excitedly.

'That's amazing honey, when is it?'

'Next month, can you come. Please. Please.'

'Oh, two pleases, I have to come now. It should be OK. Send me the details and I'll be there.'

'YES!' Tereza screeched. 'I can't believe Nic Cage is coming to my speech!'

'Very funny. How are you apart from that?'

'Good, the course is going well, I can't believe it's been three years already. Next stop Hollywood!'

'How's Ben?'

'He's good, work's going well and we're thinking of travelling to Paris this year when I finish my year.'

'Sounds great honey.'

'You're coming right?'

'Friday. I promise.'

'See you.'

'Bye.'

Getting back to police HQ, Novák made a call to the cyber intelligence unit about the IP address. It seemed it was fake and had been using a Tor browser; a kind of advanced VPN allowing it to appear anywhere and everywhere. At least the original address in Chrudim seemed to have been genuine at one time. Novák made another call to chase up the full warrant to break into the back room in the office.

Chapter 12
THE BOWLING ALLEY

The scene was set for the *event*, as it had now been named by Smutny. Despite its large size, Bowling Celnice's low ceilings gave it an underground bunker feel that no amount of bright neon lighting or wall colouring could disguise. With 6 lanes and a large canteen, there was enough space for over 300 people at any one time, and the place was already beginning to fill up nicely. Two undercover police, both with discrete earpieces were in place to make sure everything went smoothly. They casually hung about at separate ends of the club, one sipping a giant soft drink from a straw and the other selecting some bowling shoes. As luck would have it, a large coachful of British tourists from the Women's Institute was booked in for that afternoon. This, Smutny emphasised, would only add to the "authenticity halo" of the event, as the visitors communicated on mass what had happened to friends and relatives back home via social media. The discovery of the head was primarily focussed on regional and national media, but any direct international coverage would help to spread the story as far and wide as possible.

The head had been carefully placed at the base of one of the centre consoles that spat out new balls to the waiting hands of the players. Poppy Sandringham, adorned with the uniform of The WI (sky blue tennis skirt, matching socks and crisp white polo shirt), strode up to take her next ball. She was going for a heavier 14 and wasn't going to take any chances on this round, she had already been humiliated by Mary Proudspire and wasn't going to let her win this time. As she waited for a 14 to appear, Poppy limbered up by rotating her right arm in clockwise and counter-clockwise movements. Poppy was very, very competitive. She looked down, searching for the right ball but the machine began to make a strange groaning sound followed by a loud click and a pop. Noticing that one of the balls had been blocked in the aperture, she gave it a tug. It felt different from the others; strangely soft but still firm at the same time. One final pull with both hands dislodged it and she fell backwards head over heels, the object spinning in the air and arcing into a plate of exploding nachos on a nearby table. A dismembered head with a face like a chubby Yul Brynner was now staring up into the horrified faces of a family from Wisconsin. The whole place erupted and people were now running in all directions shouting 'head! head!' or 'hlava! hlava!' In the middle of the chaos, one of the undercover policemen surreptitiously took some snaps of the head, looked around and quickly munched a handful of snacks.

The screaming continued as the contents of the bowling alley emptied out into the streets. Onlookers took out their phones to capture the event. A woman screamed in an American accent to the onlookers as she pointed back to the bowling alley. A Czech family who had been inside to celebrate a 12th birthday party dragged their children up the road in shock. More onlookers stopped and filmed the spectacle. Everyone was either calling on their phones, taking photos or filming. The machine had been switched on, the genie was out of the bottle, and the head was in the nachos.

Chapter 13
THE EVIDENCE

Sitting in his dimly lit basement living room, Novák thumbed through the novel-sized book that he had found in the barn in Chrudim. It had been forwarded to his home at his request following the forensic tests which incidentally had come up with no fingerprints at all. It was as if the whole scene, including all the objects in it, had been wiped of evidence. Either that, or overalls and gloves had been used at all times when the room was being used. That in itself was evidence enough. Whoever used this room was familiar with the some of the mechanics of crime scenes or at least had some knowledge of how to decontaminate effectively. Although this was highly unusual, it wasn't the first time Novák had come across this type of situation, but he had never seen it used in relation to a murder case and it would seem to fit with the description of the man coming and going with a suitcase.

However, there was one item of evidence that astounded even Novák. A single hair had been found in the book. A hair that was estimated to be over 400 years old. He had given instructions to make inquiries into museums all over the country with strict orders to shortlist any employees with criminal records past and present. Had the book been left by accident? Surely this couldn't be a case of the "Holiday Guy" being sloppy when everything else had been so meticulously left. The book was a clue and this person liked leaving them. If he was the actual murderer or just a professional dealing in antiquities, the book had to be some kind of guide to where to look next.

Novák picked up the padded envelope and teased out the plastic zip bag that contained the hair and carefully placed the book on a side table. He held the zip bag up to the dim light cast by the reading lamp. The air was damp with a faint hint of smoke and firelighter, the light giving the room a yellow, submerged feel. A car horn blared and shook him out of this daydream. Novák picked up the book, poured a large Scotch, settled into his beaten-up leather armchair and started reading.

It followed the story of a famous Prague executioner called Jan Mydlár and it was well known in Prague. The original legend the book was based on was partly responsible for the city's reputation as a place to experience the region's dark Medieval past. Torture museums, dungeon clubs and theme restaurants had benefited from its telling and for years the municipality had been divided about whether this was good for the city or not; on the one hand it brought the tourists in, on the other it gave Prague a tacky, one dimensional image. As he read through one of the chapters, details of the legend came back to him from years of stories he had been told as a child. Jan Mydlár had been trained as a surgeon but had somehow ended up becoming the top executioner in the whole of Bohemia at the tender age of 28. The details of why he had a sudden change of career are unclear, but some said it was in connection to a tragedy that happened to his girlfriend. She had been involved in some sort of scandal and was arrested and sentenced to be executed, Jan was inconsolable and decided to quit medicine and follow the pariah life of an executioner. As Novak read on, his heart stopped. All the events had taken place in Chrudim, which had also been Mydlár's hometown. It appeared he had been the apprentice of Chrudim's master executioner and his girlfriend's scandal had happened during this time. Jan had taken possession of a powerful new Spanish sword which was said to have almost supernatural qualities. The description of the sword was identical to the one stolen from the auction house. OK, now Novák knew that someone was fucking with him.

Chapter 14
CAMPAIGN UPDATE

Operation Fake Head had already begun to gain traction on social media. The Facebook feeds of approximately 5,000 users had been infested with footage of panicked people leaving Bowling Celnice with captions like "another murder in Prague", "what's going on with this world", "These immigrants are destroying our country." To the delight of Smutny, someone had actually managed to film the head spinning into the plate of nachos and the short fuzzy clip had already been spread via Facebook, WhatsApp, Instagram, YouTube and Tik Tok even though it had been quickly blocked by social media moderators. Smutny called this "The Money Shot". An elderly lady had been trampled on and two children were badly injured in the stampede. Unfortunate, Smutny thought, but a useful detail for the sake of authenticity.

As promised, Novák arrived at the scene and was clearly visible as reporters pushed and jostled to get as close as possible to the entrance of the bowling alley. Česká Televize, Nova, ČT1, ČT24 and many other media organisations were all there. Video cameras rolled, stills cameras clicked and everything was uploaded in real time.

It was thought a press conference should not be given initially because an information vacuum only added to the media speculation, which in turn created more social media noise. In any case, Novák was highly resistant to prolonging his exposure. He had kept his end of the bargain by simply being seen at the investigation. After that, he was out.

Chapter 15
THE BOOK

Back at Novák's apartment, a call was made to chase the progress of the search warrant of the Chrudim barn. It was ready. Novák asked for the document to be emailed over. In case there were any other surprises, he decided to deal with this alone and head out discretely first thing in the morning. It would also give him time to do some more research on the Jan Mydlár story.

Novák's apartment was his refuge. The property was situated in the centre of Prague, adjacent to The Old Town Square. The tourists were annoying, but it was still a privilege to live in one of Prague's premier locations and in one of its oldest properties. It occupied the entire footprint of a Gothic building and was situated in the basement of a hotel and restaurant; what it lacked in light it more than made up for in size. Novák's daughter referred to it as his "dungeon". To him it was the only place he found peace. Novák carefully placed a fresh log in the fireplace and as the whiskey flowed and the pages turned, Jan's story became even more bizarre. As it unfolded, more and more details of Prague's history unfolded with it. The rise of The Hapsburgs, The Battle of White Mountain, The Defenestrations (whereby powerful enemies were thrown out of windows, catalysing massive sectarian conflicts). Each brutal milestone seemed to align itself perfectly with Jan's professional ascendance. A breathing sound entered the silent womb of his airless study. Now it turned into a rhythmic exhalation, increasing in speed and depth. As Novák slowly turned, he was met by the familiar face of Rudolf his Alsatian. With a grunt and a descending moan, he raised his paw and walked in the direction of the kitchen, his hint that it was time for dinner. Still reading the book, Novák walked over to the kitchen and poked around into the fridge for Rudolf's food and pulled his hand back in pain. He had found the food can, and the sharp edge of the can had found his finger. Pulling it out carefully over to the sink, he turned on the tap to try to stop the blood from going everywhere. Meanwhile Rudolf licked his lips noisily and sat up in a regimented stance. As Rudolf devoured his food, the metal bowl scraped along the stone floor. It was always the way that by the time he had licked every morsel, the bowl ended up on the other side of the kitchen floor and Rudolf looked up and cocked his head as if to say "Hey, how did that happen?". With a kitchen cloth wrapped around his finger and the book balanced in his hand, Novák filled Rudolf's water bowl and the whole moving bowl dance began once again. Novák read on.

It seemed that Jan Mydlár's rise to fame reached its apex in 1621 when he had executed 27 dissidents in just one day. This had sealed his fate as not only the most famous executioner in Prague but the most infamous executioner in Medieval history. The men to be executed were Protestants at the centre of a failed attempt to seize power at The Battle of White Mountain and the executions had been a catalyst for the 30 years' war. By all accounts, this particular display of judicial enforcement had been a bit of an event. The whole of Bohemia was given a day off to ensure it would be remembered forever. The area where The Old Town Square is now, was where all high-profile executions took place and the ruling Hapsburgs wanted to make an example of these men. At least 7 were high profile noblemen and 12 of the 27 were executed by decapitation to maximise the optics. Jan was even told to remove their fingers and place them in their mouths to enhance the humiliation. The heads of the 12 were placed in bird cages and hung on either side of Charles Bridge and left to rot for years as reminder of that day. Jan had himself been a Protestant and he had made sure his swords were as sharp as possible so the executions would be swift and painless. Some of the men were also publicly tortured in various gruesome ways, but again, because Mydlár was a surgeon he knew how to minimise the pain of his victims. That is, when he chose to; some of the victims had been high profile aristocrats.

"...some say that Jan Mydlár had even relished this aspect of the day's proceedings. After all, it was a scurrilous rumour spread by an aristocrat about Dorota being a witch, that had finally sealed her fate..."

This was an unprecedented reminder that no one was untouchable, and the people of Bohemia had been divided about this line that had been crossed.

Novák walked up and out of his apartment into the chilly air for a break. The streets were silent except for the sound of a local bar owner pulling down the shutters for the night. As he stretched his back and looked up, Novák noticed an ironing board propped against the window of a brightly lit upper window, the folded legs poking up above the end of the board like antennas on a head, giving the silhouette a distinctly insect-like quality. It seemed to be staring directly down at him. Returning to the dungeon, the fire cracked, and a blue puff of smoke rose into the air and floated towards him. He reached through his shirt and pulled out the pendant hanging around his chest. Surely there couldn't be some religious psychopath on the rampage in Prague. If there was, and the killer was also following Jan Mydlár's story, then more innocent people would be killed. Tomorrow the Chrudim barn would hopefully reveal some more evidence. Time for a nightcap.

Chapter 16
FAKE HEAD PHASE TWO

It had been 3 days since the event in the bowling alley and social media had gone into overdrive. The clips had now been shared 2 million times and the event had already been seen by an estimated 5 million people worldwide. A press conference was arranged in front of The Astronomical Clock in The Old Town Square. The low sun gave the ancient brickwork of the building a pale orange hue. As a small stage and sound system were being set up, various public officials nervously shuffled about, some smoking, some texting on their phones. Jacob Smutny lurked in the shadows to the side of the stage. This time CNN, Fox, BBC, France 24, ZDF as well as all the regional news outlets were present.

As the press congregated, the atmosphere was hysterical. The public had turned up in their thousands, and people were shouting abusive comments towards the group of officials waiting for the appointed time. A cordon had been erected in order to keep the public back and the whole scene resembled a sequence from a Frankenstein movie, except this time, fiery torches and lederhosen were replaced with mobile phones and hoodies. As the public official carefully tapped the mike, it let out a squawk of feedback as he approached the podium. He pulled out a small piece of paper of notes. He was clearly uncomfortable.

'Thank you all for coming today, and thank you for your patience. This has been a difficult time for our city, but we have some more news about the events that took place at Bowling Celnice last week and I am glad to say the news is good.' With that, a voice shouted something about killing terrorists, causing a ripple effect which in turn activated more noise from the crowd. Soon enough, everyone began shouting about their particular grievances, whether related to the incident or not. The official shouted 'It would seem, we have been misled'. The ripple of grievance began to subside as his eyes glanced down to his script.

'Last night, following thorough scientific tests, our forensic team has concluded that the dismembered body part was in fact fake, and it seems', he hesitated, 'We have been the victim of some kind of practical joke.'

Gradually, like a trickle of water slowly coming out of a tap, a giggle began to fill the air. Soon the trickle turned into a torrent and the entire crowd was falling around laughing. The official now had to shout to be heard. 'For now, we will be focussing on the original murder and the investigation will be…' But these words were drowned out by the cacophony of uncontrollable laughter and the sound of the world's press calling in or texting back to their media overlords.

Back in Prague HQ, Jacob Smutny's spindly fingers typed into his laptop.

#Fakehead

Within minutes, 200 primed Facebook and Twitter accounts started using the hashtag. Ten 'independent' travel sites were launched and began releasing content related to Prague with the hashtag. Booking.com had already created a severed head icon to highlight #Fakehead deals to Prague. On YouTube, Instagram and TikTok, memes were created featuring homemade videos of fake heads being planted and discovered in people's homes and public places. A new hashtag was created (this time by real users). They called it #Fakeheading. Fakeheading was entered onto the list for inclusion into the Merriam-Webster and Oxford English dictionaries for that year.

The studio of BBC Newsnight was the backdrop to the latest discussion on the matter. Representatives from The Labour Party and The Conservatives slugged it out from their own obliquely irrelevant perspectives, moral decline from The Conservatives, lack of social mobility from Labour.

'... It's the whole Fakehead culture, I mean honestly. Do you think this is something our children should be involved in? When a video clip of a prosthetic head in a toilet being discovered by a grandad is shared by 2 million people, you really have to wonder how it's come to this.'

A TV show was pitched to Channel 4 called Celebrity Fakehead, where Z listers would compete to create the best clay heads and find the most original place to hide them in the grounds of a 17th Century mansion in the Cotswolds. To date #Fakehead had been shared 9.7 million times. Over 20 million page impressions that included Fakeheading had been launched. YouTube had spawned hundreds of Fakeheading fan video pages. TikTok temporally shut down with an overload of traffic to one of its pages. Prague had been inundated with tourists, hotel bookings were unusually high for the season and the song by Czech Death Metal band Axiom called 'Fakehead is my Home' was the most streamed song globally for that month on Spotify, Apple Music, Tidal, Deezer and Amazon.

A hideous, purple, bluish light entered Novák's living room. A faint hissing mingled with sounds of laughing children and buried screams accompanied brightly coloured images of decapitated, decomposed heads. Smashing inward, a kaleidoscope of spinning boxes appeared, disappeared and froze in place. The sounds vibrated in unison as the apparitions repeated again in nightmarish convulsions. Giant teeth, smiling, grimacing, gnawing. The loop began again like waves of nausea rising and spraying forth its hellish neon vomit - the brightly lit studio of the Fox News team burst onto the TV. Novák woke with a thudding heart, his whiskey glass falling to the floor into a hundred pieces. The cheerily robotic female host, all blonde bouffant, bright teeth and war-paint, announces as the revolving graphics fly forward with a violent swooshing sound towards the screen.

'Now to Prague, where someone is certainly getting over their head. Our Eastern European anchor, Ted Malveny has a report on the latest on the head situation'.

'Ted?'.

'Thanks Cathy. At 9am EET the Czech authorities gave a press briefing in relation to a grisly murder that supposedly happened a few days ago. But there is a twist. According to officials, the head that was found in a popular bowling alley here in central Prague was in fact fake. No other comments have been made. However, a video has been released of police officials displaying the head outside their headquarters following the public announcement'.

Another swooshing graphic box presented a video showing the head being lifted and displayed in three different positions for the waiting photographers and journalists outside the Městská Policie Headquarters.

'What's incredible Cathy is that this usually quiet, genteel town has never experienced anything quite like this and earlier this year, there was a worry that the killings could be Al Qaeda or ISIS related. As you know Cathy, the social media attention around this event has been almost overwhelming for the authorities here but it seems, for now at least, the good people of Prague can sleep easy'.

'Cathy'.

'Thanks Ted'.

'And now from heads to *beds*. A small town in Northern California, has a problem with bed bugs. Our nature reporter Katie Newman reports from Oakland ...'

Chapter 17
THE BARN AT CHRUDIM

Novák turned in to the town square at Chrudim. The early afternoon sky was bright, and the sun bounced its rays straight to his developing headache in the back of his eyes. Donning sunglasses he lurched out of his car and made his way up the narrow street towards the barn. A local officer was there to meet him, Novák showed her the warrant on his phone and they mounted the metal steps to the office. Police tape had been placed over the door and the officer pulled it back for them to enter. Moving straight for the locked door to the right, the officer removed her equipment from a black sports bag. A selection of bolt cutters, hammers and an electric metal cutter was removed. As the officer went to work, Novák looked around the now brightly lit room for any more answers. It was just as he had left it but the smell seemed different. Tiny galaxies of floating dust bobbed around in the fading sun as the electric saw ground away, throwing sparks backwards and downwards in bright blue dots and flashes. It didn't take long for the door lock to give and the officer gave it one last hammer and the door flew in. As they entered the windowless room they were met with a strong stench, both Novák and the officer held their hands up to their faces involuntarily. Their torches cast light in every corner of the space. The room was empty and airless as if all life had been sucked out of it long ago. As the officer moved slowly forward, her boot collided with a lump on the floor. She cast her torch below, to expose a rough brown sack about 6-foot long. Novák held his hand up for her to wait, and the officer picked out a crowbar from the sports bag and handed it to Novák. Gently poking down, the crowbar met resistance. Carefully pulling back a fold of sacking, revealed a blackness of almost artificial depth. It seemed to shimmer as their torchlights bounced unevenly across the surfaces of the object. The smell became worse as a large dead eye stared up at them. As the layers of cloth were unpeeled, several large black birds came into view. There must have been five of them in the bag. Maggots busily went about their wriggling, maggoty business as the stench rose to a crescendo. Novák poked down lightly into the mass of feathers. A deadened metallic sound rang out. He tapped again and flipped back one of the wings to show a large reflective object underneath the black, avian cemetery. They both applied latex gloves and carefully heaved away the rotting corpses. It was the missing executioner's sword, its distinctive snake patterned handle undulating under the dim torchlight. A call was made for a local forensics team to arrive immediately. Pointing his torch across the length of the room to the far end, there seemed to be a concrete wall. A faint rectangular line the size of a door could just about be seen by the torch's bright beam. A request was made for a heavy demolition team to come to open the place up ASAP.

Novák had put in a priority request to get the evidence tested and managed to pull some favours back at Prague HQ. They had expedited a 12-hour turnaround with the local forensics in Chrudim. Maybe they were taking this seriously at long last. He would personally oversee the forensics team so it was looking like it was going to be a long day. As he searched for somewhere to stay locally, an alert sounded on his phone. It was a reminder for Tereza's event at the film school. The idea of some psychopath walking around anywhere near his daughter sickened him to his stomach. He would be keeping an even closer eye on her in the coming weeks. He reset the alert and searched for a hotel and managed to get a last-minute room on Booking.com using something called a #Fakehead Deal.

The forensics team arrived one hour later and laid out their kit in neat lines. The team assessed the carrion for its cause of death and lividity and the sword was swabbed in situ for blood and DNA. Luminol was used to identify any blood stains hidden by the darkness. Needless to say, the whole scene lit up like some kind of conceptual sculpture, the surreal images remaining behind Novák's retinas with each pop and flash of the camera. The animals were removed carefully and place into individual evidence bags. There were 7 in total. The liquid samples were placed in tiny testing vials to be matched by the central database in the morning.

Chapter 18
THE RABBIT HOLE

As Novák pulled into the wooded area next to the hotel, the pressure dropped like a stone. A raven sign hanging above the hotel swung in the wind, the stiff metal scraping against metal seemed to bring the bird to life, its upward pointed beak screeching to the sky. Leaves like giant brown insects flew around in mini tornados around the pub entrance as the muffled syncopations of an accordion melody floated out of the pub. As he stepped into the dark entrance, he was blocked by a bulky figure wearing a Medieval cloak, executioner's mask and carrying an axe. Novák's mind was elsewhere so his initial instinct was to reach for his sidearm. Noticing his reaction, a muffled laugh came from the man, and with an apology he stood aside to let him in. Inside, it looked like there was a party being prepared, guests in Medieval costumes were already gyrating on the dancefloor to the accordion player as the dj was setting up his decks. As he checked in, he looked to his left down the dark hall of the ground floor hotel and noticed beer kegs being placed into the cellar in preparation for the night's revelries. That same pressure change he had felt in the joke shop in Nerudova Street tugged at his ears now. The cellars. The whole of Prague contained miles of tunnels spreading out like veins in a human body. They had been the dwellings of previous generations, and the city had simply been built on top of them following centuries of successive flooding from the river Vltava. That must have been how the head had been placed in the shop without any sign of entry. The case was finally falling into place piece by piece. He made a call to the owner of the auction house to inform him that his sword had been found and that he would be returning it to him tomorrow first thing.

That night, the thumping continued, reverberating relentlessly through the walls of the hotel as Novák tried to sleep. No wonder there had been a free room. He looked at his watch - 2:30am. Rather than attempting to sleep, he decided on the medicinal route, was dressed and down to the bar by 2:33 where the party was in full swing. Revellers dressed as skeletons, maidens, noblemen, peasants and executioners were getting down on the dance floor to the EDM belting out from a sound system so large it was almost comical in relation to the size of the old pub. The brass fittings on the bar jangled in unison with the cavernous bass line and Novák was confronted by a grotesque pig's head carving over the bar as he lowered his head and shouted his order of a double Johnny Walker straight up. Looking around for somewhere to sit, he noticed an area through a low beamed arch that was conspicuous by its absence of cosplay. His way was blocked by yet another masked executioner. He pushed past and sat, took a good slug of whiskey and started to type on his phone.

Hey you
Just a quick catch up to see how you are
Out of town on a work assignment
Be back in the morning
Really looking forward to the talk next week
Dad
PS. I hope you're not still up, it's late!

Just as he pressed send, a girl with a Medieval pointed hat knocked into his table and fell towards him onto his drink. With lighting reflexes, he saved the glass from being spilled. The girl recoiled back upwards, apologized and then started staring at him.

With a slurring voice and eyeballs independently rotating at 180-degree angles, she introduced herself.

'Hey, don't I know you?'

'No you don't, I'm not him.' Novák went back to his phone.

'Who?'

'Never mind, get back to your party.'

'What party?'

Novák pointed in the direction of the music.

'Oh yeah.'

Laughing maniacally, she turned and winked at him before floating away in a waft of diaphanous nylon and skunk weed.

Novák was planning his next move on the case. First thing in the morning, the auctioneers. He'd return the sword and make some more enquiries about the night of the theft. There must have been something he'd missed and now there was at least a chance the item was connected to the murders, he had to probe even further. Returning the sword in person gave him a chance to ingratiate himself with the auction house owner, who let's face it hadn't been exactly helpful first-time round. Knocking back the last dregs of whiskey, he headed to the bar for (another) nightcap. As he stood, he felt a lump between his teeth and poked his finger in to retrieve the object. It had been firmly lodged between his canine and molar and he moved his tongue around to dislodge it. Twisting his tongue round, he pulled at it. It looked like a rolled-up piece of paper. Unravelling it with his thumb and forefinger he squinted down. It was only about 5 millimeters square with something printed on it. Peering down in the ambient candlelight, the image flickered into view - a deep purple executioner symbol with two tiny dots for eyes. Throwing it to the floor in disgust he made his way to the bar and ordered another JW, as the chaos of the costume party unfolded around him, the bass drum's metronomic pattern and syncopated high hat defining each passing second.

As he lent on the bar sipping his whiskey, he began to feel slight nausea in the pit of his stomach and heading back to his table he exhaled and sat. Gradually, the nausea started to be replaced by a feeling of gentle warmth. The whiskey was beginning to work its magic. As he closed his eyes, the distant rhythmic thump next door seemed to be in sync with the rhythm of the pulse behind his eyes, now waves of pleasure started to flow over his head and down his spine and back again. Looking at the whiskey within his glass revealed so much more than liquid. It was nourishment, waves from the sea, milk from the sea. He sipped again and the heat of the liquid seemed to wrap his throat in a warm velvet glove of security and... what was it. Love? Yes, love. Whiskey was love. He loved it. It loved him. It was all about love and mind. Whiskey, love and mind. He noticed a mirror in the far distance of the quiet area. It reflected a flickering fireplace that he hadn't noticed before. Looking behind him only revealed a white wall. At first this alarmed him, but then slowly he began to laugh quietly to himself, then gradually out loud, until the whole space was filled with it as it bounced around the low-ceilinged space. He looked back to the fireplace but it was gone and immediately he needed to pee. He felt unsteady on his feet, unsteady yet full of energy, light and bouncy like a brand-new tennis ball. Laughing at the thought of comparing himself to a tennis ball, he staggered carefully towards the men's bathroom.

The bathroom's dark red decor seemed like the inside of a giant, moist vagina. This aesthetic decision struck him as making total sense as he nodded, unzipped and started to pee. The feeling of relief was almost orgasmic as he gave out a long deep grown. The sound of his voice and the liquid expulsion echoed around the bathroom, the tiles seemed to amplify every tone and sound in bright, clear waves. Crystal. Boundless. Sonically pure. After what seemed like hours, he finally finished, zipped up his fly and bounced to the sink. Pressing down the taps, the feeling of water on his hands felt delicious, his hands surrounded by warm, slippery soap, the smell, feminine like lavender and rose. Meanwhile, the walls of the bathroom seemed to be pulsating in time with the distant bass drum. Why hadn't he noticed how fun handwashing could be before? Noticing a broken towel dispenser (which suddenly made him sad) he turned to the first private cubicle for some paper. The light was dim, but he noticed it had its own light switch. He flicked it on and there he saw it emblazoned on the back wall of the cubicle in black marker pen.

Those who are liars are sure to be found
Taken by sword or burial ground
I will relive the death of my Dorota
On Saint Lucas Day 18th of October

He almost dropped his phone into the toilet as he fumbled with the buttons and took several photos. He thought he imagined the engine of a motorbike speeding away. Rushing out of the bathroom, he pushed his way through the crowded dance floor, past the carved pig who was now laughing at him, and through the smoke machine fog that was belching out multicoloured clouds from the dancefloor out into the corridors of the pub. Skeletons dancing with sweating executioners, waving hands and shuffling feet moved in time with the pounding bass drum and the incessant click clack of the high hat.

Running out of the pub, gasping for air he immediately noticed flashing lights coming from the woods. Running towards his car he noticed the emergency lights were flashing but there was no alarm. The front window had been smashed in and the alarm system had been disabled. Running to the back of the car he flipped up the lid. The carefully wrapped and concealed sword was gone.

Chapter 19
RETURN OF THE JAN

Charles bridge stretched out in front of Jan Mydlár. It was as if he was walking out of the open mouth of a fantastical creature. The foggy cobbled road like the tongue, the statues on either side like rows of jagged teeth silhouetted against the blood red sunset.

His six and a half foot frame filled the space around him, red cloak flapping in the breeze, the heels of his boots echoed along the cobble stones. Small, strange looking metallic carriages on tiny wheels, in dizzying arrays of colours moved around the streets at such a fast pace, he had to keep looking in every direction not to get hit by them. They were somehow propelled without horse and were accompanied by a roaring, buzzing sound that came from within. The noise of these machines and the sheer number of people in the city was bewildering. Magic lights that seemed to burn without a flame were everywhere. There were no horses in sight. The smell, unfamiliar, a burning, alchemic smell, astringent, oppressive. Shouts were directed at him to get out of the way, their dialect familiar but unusual for the Bohemian lands. He knew public opinion of him was divided, but people had never been this aggressive or rude towards him before. Everyone seemed to be muttering to themselves as they walked in the street, particularly those who wore a strange form of white jewellery connected to their ears. Passing a trader of books, he noticed a large sign saying "Flat Earth. Flat Out Truth". Jan had had many heated arguments in the tavern with these uneducated imbeciles who believed the world to be flat. How they could still be talking of such nonsense now in the 17th Century was beyond him.

He had no memory of where he had been or indeed where he was going. The only thing he did know was that he was looking for an important possession, the most important possession of his whole life. The Spanish sword, given to him by master Jirí when he had passed away had become a talisman for him of sorts (in as much as someone as unlucky as Jan Mydlár could ever have a talisman). His infamy had been intimately linked with it, and to this end, his superstition about it had become almost obsessional. That was why, when it went missing from his mansion last night, he knew it had to be found.

He also had another compulsion. Murder.

Although his job, which one could argue, was that of a professional murderer and had involved a great deal of it, it was always undertaken with the detachment of professionalism and judicial duty.

No, this feeling was different. It felt. Personal. It was like an itch that wouldn't go away. An itch in his mind. In one way rational, in another uncontrollable with rage.

Ever since he had to commit the awful deed, it had eaten away at him. His executioner's career had been one prolonged displacement activity, and when he retired, it had left a gaping hole in his heart. A gaping hole in the ground had consumed his love on that fateful day in October and it felt like he had been waiting hundreds of years for this moment.

But should it be revenge or re-enactment? Repeating The Deed made more sense to him as his brain wriggled and squirmed in approval. A burial of another maiden. Yes. This would exorcize the event in his mind. Repeating it again and again made it acceptable, made the real act fade away, seem less significant. It made it all better. But. Revenge. How would *this* be achieved?

Novák floored the accelerator back to Prague, pushing the car's engine as hard as he could. Although the LSD had begun to wear off, he still had a jittery feeling combined with an empty-headed looseness that made driving a challenge. He had to get back to his apartment to match the toilet graffiti with any information in the book that could finally lead him to the killer. The sun was beginning to rise, the shapes of the trees starting to poke out on the edge of the orange horizon like little dancing skeletons. He called Tereza's phone from his handsfree button, the dialling tone deafening in the car. There was no answer.

He pulled into his underground parking bay and almost ran over the parking attendant in the process. Leaping out and running to the lift, he impatiently pressed the ground floor button. As the lift finally arrived, a family slowly started to exit with luggage in tow. One of the bags had got stuck in the back of the lift and Novák moved in to help, pulling it out and wheeling it out of the lift as the mother gestured a nod of thanks. Checking his watch, Novák pressed the button and waited, arms folded. Exiting the lift at the ground floor a large shape caught his eye. A man dressed as a Medieval executioner, red cloak, arms folded, was standing outside with his back to the glass exit door. Novák pushed out into the street as the executioner's phone rang, he pulled his mask off and answered with a broad American accent. Running towards his apartment on U Radnice, Novák walked straight into a cyclist, as he tumbled into a passing car, the driver swerved, narrowly missing another passer-by. As he approached the low sets of arches outside his apartment, he hit Tereza's number. No answer.

The hulking shape of Rudolf on his hind legs could be seen through the stained glass as he unlocked and entered. Placing some fresh water and food out for of him, he headed for the living room to retrieve the book. As he flipped through the images on his phone and skimmed through the dense pages, a number stood out near where he had marked his last place. October 18th. This had been the day that Jan Mydlár had buried Dorota in front of the crowd in Chrudim. Novák sat down slowly, the blood drained from his face, his heart pounding with panic. Tonight was October the 18th and was the night of Tereza's speech at the university. Just as he put the phone down it rang. It was Tereza.

'Hey, what's up, you called about 3 times and I got your text just now, is everything OK?'

'Yes, all good, just wishing you luck for tonight.'

'Dad, are you OK, your voice sounds funny.'

'No, just a little tired honey.'

'OK, you're still going to make it tonight though, right?'

'I wouldn't miss it for the world.'

'OK, see you later. Remember I'm on at about 9.30, don't be late.'

'Tereza?'

'Dad?'

'Just...'

'Just, what?'

'Just...good luck. Have a great night. See you later.'

As he sat in the darkness, fatigue enveloped him like a warm cloak and pulled him down into a deep, dark sleep. A dreamless, dead sleep, except for the soft sound of earth on shovel, stone on mud.

Tomáš Novák woke with a start. The time was 4.05, he had 3 missed calls on his phone. None were from Tereza. He had enough time to look at the report from Chrudim before heading to Tereza's speech. He poured a whiskey and downed it in one and headed to the bedroom at the back of the apartment. The large space was minimal and tidy, dark hardwood cabinets flanked the bed and a large chest of drawers faced it. Opening the lower drawer, he reached to the back and pulled out his knife with leg holster and threw it on the bed, a knuckle duster was secreted in the inside of his suit jacket.

Suited up, as he petted Rudolf he started to growl quietly. Novák looked past his stare in the direction of the front of the apartment and switched off the living room lights, kept silent and placed his forefinger over his mouth to gesture to Rudolf to do the same. The animal was clearly uncomfortable and persisted with his groaning. A car with a heavy bass sound system was parked in the street and it rattled the pictures inside the apartment like a rhythmic earthquake. So much chaos in this once peaceful city, it really was time to move out and live the quiet life. Out in the street, Novák double-locked the front door and quickly turned in the direction of the underground parking lot as Rudolf stood up on his back legs and did his tap-dancing routine on the inside of the door. The wind seemed to be picking up and the last of the autumn sun dipped below The Old Town Square as drinkers were beginning to fill up the areas outside the various overpriced bars. A few fancy dress revellers were already out and about for the latest round of bachelor and bachelorette parties. Fog was already beginning to slip over Charles Bridge and lie in wispy clumps along the street. Novák entered the ground level parking lot and headed for the lift. Just as the lift opened, he got a new text. It was from the team in Chrudim and contained multiple attachments. The images were slightly unclear but he could make out multiple faces. Heads were featured on what looked like columns or plinths, in the way sculptures were displayed in a museum. As he scrolled through the images, he moved towards his parking spot.

The brief message read:
5 prosthetic heads
1 pot of artificial blood
2 wooden antique Czech puppets with real hair (estimated 16th Century)
1 large brown suitcase
1 trilby hat
WTF?

Smutny. Now it all made sense. He put a call through to the Prague forensics department.

'Hi, this is Tomáš Novák, could you put me through to Eliška Černý please.'

The phone clicked briefly. The operator came back on the line.

'Mr Novák, sorry could you give me that name again please.'

'Eliška Černý, she has been at the forensics department for the past 5 years.'

The phone clicked once more.

'Sir, according to our records, she resigned two weeks ago.'

Novák hung up.

As he clicked the car entry key with an electronic chirp, he noticed a presence behind him. It was the tourist dressed as an executioner he had seen earlier. He seemed taller this time, in fact this man was huge. Funny he hadn't noticed that before.

'Isn't there a party you should be at?'

The figure just stood still.

'Look if you don't move, I'll have to call it in'.

He reached for his Police ID.

In a split second, a forearm the size of a man's calf shot out from beneath the red cloak and grabbed his wrist. Instinctively, Novák reached for his automatic sidearm. Jan Mydlár knocked it out of his hand and sent it skidding along the concrete floor under the car. Novák ducked and reached for the knife strapped to his leg and stabbed Mydlár in the lower leg, pulled out the blade and stabbed again just above the knee. As if this had no effect whatsoever, Mydlár reached down and pulled Novák up, carrying him by his arms and broke them both at the elbows with a sound like a snapping chicken leg (Mydlár estimated this was achieved by popping the Capitulum in the left, and cracking the Olecranon of the Ulna in the right). One of his bones had ripped through his suit jacket. As Novák screamed out in pain he kicked Mydlár in the chest with both legs, almost taking him off balance. Mydlár dropped Novák and punched him in the wind-pipe. As he choked and pulled his head back to try to breathe, his Protestant pendant with its falling bird symbol caught the light and reflected into Jan Mydlár's eyes. Novák collapsed into a heap of blood and bones onto the concrete floor as the fog crept down the exit runway enveloping him in icy tendrils. Mydlár forced open the boot of Novak's car. As the lid flipped up, a flock of ravens came pouring out in a thick smog of black feathers and clapping beaks. Its velocity and volume increased, turned into a vertical, gravity-defying black liquid, pouring upwards and over the car park's low ceiling until it spread like an avian oil slick out of the exit. As the last birds fluttered out of the boot, Mydlár bent over it, inhaled the air through his nostrils, turned and followed the sea of ravens streaming out into the street.

Chapter 20
THE HOTEL

Dim streetlamps illuminated deposits of shiny, cold moisture on the paving stones leading up to The Alchymist Grand Hotel, its tastefully lit entrance making it stand out at the top of the lane. The faint smell of an open fireplace seemed to waft directly out of its arched entrance as well as the strains of Vivaldi. Darius Marcus parked his Ducati, dismounted carefully and unstrapped the long, heavy package from the side of his bike. Seeing as it looked like some kind of thin, black mummified corpse, he thought it better to avoid the conspicuous front entrance, and enter incognito. He made his way to the side of the hotel and ascended the gently sloping alley, and pushing through the wooden door revealed an interior garden with bulky cone-shaped topiary distributed at neat intervals across the now dark landscape. They looked like giant overweight sentinels as Darius' eyes slowly adjusted to the dark. As he squinted to look for the side door to re-enter the hotel, he thought he noticed movement in one of the bushes and stopped. The breeze picked up, and lightly rustled the plastic packaging of the sword. One of the bushy sentinels seemed to slowly change shape and move towards him from behind. Sensing this, he turned and faced what looked like a fancy dress monk. A very large, bulky fancy dress monk. The smell of woodsmoke was suddenly overpowered by patchouli and damp earth. Darius instinctively laughed, but sensing something was very wrong indeed, turned and ran in the direction he had come from, knocking over a brass planter as he burst through the door back into the side alley. Instead of turning right he darted left, further up the alley into the darkness. Jan Mydlár was right behind him, his size incongruous with the speed and agility of his movements. Darius turned right into another alley and ran further up into the small labyrinth of streets behind the hotel. The street curved left again and he looked in horror at the large double gate blocking his way at the end of the alley. Pulling desperately at the lock, he looked back as Mydlár came hurtling up the alley towards him. Darius ran back to take a long jump to try to climb over the gate even though it was topped with viciously pointed spikes, but he was not quick enough and Mydlár pulled him back, ripping his coat from his back as if it were made of paper. All Darius could do was cower on the ground on his knees, face covered, with his back to the gate.

'Here, I'll give you anything, money? Here.'

He handed his wallet bulging with Euros.

Mydlár just stood silent.

Darius unclasped his watch and pathetically passed it up, trembling.

'It's a one one-off. Patek Philippe. Probably worth...'

Mydlár grabbed the watch, crushed it into a metallic ball, raised his massive right palm to elicit silence and then pointed to the sword.

With trembling hands, Darius reached down beside him and lifted the black plastic package up towards Mydlár.

Like serpent's eyes suddenly opening after a long slumber, the holes at the tip of the sword opened in hungry anticipation.

Chapter 21
THE HOSPITAL

Carrying a huge bunch of flowers, Jacob Smutny approached the front desk of the Na Homolce Hospital. He was led along the corridor to the last door on the right. Opening the door to the private room, revealed Tomáš Novák lying in bed with both his arms in casts and suspended by supports. Smutny giggled.

'Man you look rough.' He giggled nervously again.

All Novák could do was nod and grunt, his larynx had been destroyed and he was booked in for weeks of speech therapy.

'Well you really came through bro. Tourists are back. Everyone's already forgotten about the murders. Or should I say murders.'

Smutny made quote marks around that last word and giggled once more.

'The best bit was you didn't even know the first two murders were also fake.'

'Gotcha!'

Smutny pointed two fingers at Novák, the way a kid pretends to point a gun.

'#Fakehead has even won some advertising awards. It's all good bud.' Just then, the phone rang.

'Sorry, I've just got to get this.'

His gold signet ring caught the light as he held his phone to speak.

Very *aristocratic,* Novák thought.

Smutny ended the call. 'Sorry about that.'

'All you need to know is everything is safe now. You did your bit. All's good bud.' He slapped Novák gently on his leg.

Novák grunted two syllables.

'Oh, you mean the forensic. Oh, she was easy. Yeah, she wasn't happy in her job. We gave her early retirement, sealed with an NDA. She's in erm...'

Smutny scrolled on his phone.

'Hawaii. Nice!'

'We had a pretty good budget.'

Novák grunted even louder. This time with three syllables.

'What's that bud?'

Novák was beginning to get even more agitated.

'The department is pulling out the stops to find the guy who attacked you by the way. Something happened over in Tržiště. Some guy was found screaming to himself about a huge monk with a sword. Very strange. Anyway all leads are being followed up, as they say.'

More agitation from Novák, who was now moving his legs energetically.

'Anywho, I've gotta split. Rest up and you'll be back in the saddle in no time.'

With that, Smutny looked around the sparce room for somewhere to place the flowers and dumped them upside down in the bathroom sink, looked back to his phone's screen, turned and left the room.

Chapter 22
FILM SCHOOL

The student crowd, already refreshed by the free beer and vodka, were enthusiastically whooping and clapping as Tereza Novák stood down from the podium. She tried to hide her disappointment as she craned her neck and stood on tip toes to see all the way to the back of the auditorium, looking from right to left. She stepped off the stage, smiled modestly and gave a sarcastic bow for extra effect. On the surface she was happy. But underneath? She was used to disappointment, used to being let down, but she was also an expert at hiding her feelings. She was an expert at acting like everything was OK, all was going to plan.

However, even though she had those very feelings about her father once more, the anger was tinged with worry. Call it intuition. Maybe it was the way he had sounded on the phone last time they spoke. Moving back to her seat she fumbled in the bottom of her bag and fished out her phone and pressed send. The phone once more went through to voicemail.

Jan Mydlár stood in the shadows at the back of the large auditorium. His breathing calm but heavy. He had hardly believed his eyes as he looked upon Tereza talking from the podium. The way she moved her long blonde hair away from her face and placed it behind her left ear in between words, the way she skipped back with both hands behind her back and paused between paragraphs of her speech. Everything about her was the same. The itch started to scratch and the scratch started to pull. Tonight would be the night, The Deed would be completed.

Outside the auditorium, Tereza's friends had spent the last 10 minutes trying to convince her to go to the after party. She declined politely once more and thanked everyone, zipped up her coat and made her way alone down Pštrossova Street. The narrow, graffiti covered thoroughfare was empty except for the small crowd of students noisily exiting the college building and their voices slowly faded away into the distance. She liked times like these. Alone time. Quiet. Positively reflecting on the day. The talk had gone better than expected, and her tutor had complimented her (better late than never). But the thought of her dad had begun to creep up and pull her down again, and she thought of trying to call him one more time. The wind whistled down the narrow alley and blew a solitary, red plastic bag in graceful pirouettes from side to side. As she started to write a text, a strange smell came out of nowhere. Similar to damp mud or rotten incense. She felt a tap on her shoulder and quickly turned but there was no one there. Turning again, she noticed someone behind her.

'Waaaaaaaah.'

Came the sound of an inebriated fellow student, Kristof. He had been trying to get into her pants for the whole year and now the course was over, it was his last chance.

'Hello, Kristof.' She retorted, coolly.

'Pleeeeeaase come out with us, we need to ceraaabate.'

'Haven't you done enough "cerabating" already Kristof.'
'No. No. Definarly. No.'

'Goodnight Kristof. I'll see you on Insta. You've got my number. Keep in touch.'

With that, Tereza walked off as she looked down at her phone. The red plastic bag seemed to follow her like a loyal dog, as she wound down the lane back to her home on the other side of town.

But, dear reader. The story does not end there because it must end with The Deed.

We know Jan Mydlár is not an evil man. He was the victim of circumstance. Circumstances beyond his control. How can we blame him for acting in an irrational way, when faced with such irrational choices on that night in 1586?

There are always choices; should the death be slow and painful? Fast and merciful? Vengeful. These are the only choices Jan had now, as his eyes twitched and his brain wriggled, weighing up the various options.

And so, on this night of the 18th of October 2022 Jan Mydlár slowly approached Dorota on Pštrossova Street. A life unfolded before him. University began. The summer days with Uncle Mathew were starting once more. It felt like the beginning of a new journey that was also somehow familiar, as if in a re-occurring dream; a new life being lived but every detail already known. Jan felt a sense of warm security that all was not lost. No more fighting. No more good. No more bad. Today was a good day. He could see the years stretching out ahead of him. Beyond the bleak horizon of night. Beyond even his own hopes and dreams. Tonight was the beginning of forever.

Yes, there are always choices...

Chapter 23
CHARLES BRIDGE

Morning light began to punctuate the darkness of the low arches with its cafes and eateries opening up for the day. Past the U Mecenáše Restaurant sign (with ubiquitous axe hanging), and walking out of the arches, a bright blue penetrating sky came into view. It was late April and peak season, so the Malá Strana district was bustling with tourists. Four 1920s style red limousines were lined on the edges of Mostecká, their podgy drivers having iced coffee breaks before their shifts started. The atmosphere, gentle and relaxed. As the road narrowed slightly, the azure contrasted with the dark brickwork of the fortified arch leading to Charles Bridge. Tomáš Novák, standing with Rudolf was posing with two ice creams in front of the arch. Tereza repeated promiňte, promiňte, when she almost knocked over an old lady as she stepped back to take the photo with her phone. It was just another day in the life of a father and daughter.

Jacob Smutny was also there. His eyes looked out across the Vltava, high up, looking far into the distance. Looking, but not seeing. Seeing but not conscious.

From within a birdcage, placed in a central position over the arch facing Charles Bridge, was his severed head. His face looked comically surprised with its rictus grin and wide staring eyes. His own finger (still wearing the gold signet ring, naturally) was stuffed in his mouth. Tomáš and Tereza didn't even notice the head as they laughed, walking out of the arch onto the bridge. In fact, it had been ignored for months as it was thought to be just another part of the theatrics of Prague's charm, mere street theatre. After all, who would care about a fake head in a bird cage? Thanks to Jacob Smutny, Prague had seen it all before.

And so the light was altered once more, but this time it was not the light being violently extinguished but a candle gently illuminating a room. Shedding light upon lies and exposing truth. They say that if you are good at lying, you don't need to be good at anything else. The trouble is the truth will catch up with you eventually.

But what of Jan Mydlár I hear you say? That story is for another day.

Printed in Great Britain
by Amazon